DEADMAN'S LAMENT

(THE DEADMAN BOOK 1)

LINELL JEPPSEN

WOLFPACK
PUBLISHING
— EST 2013 —

Deadman's Lament
(The Deadman Book 1)

Paperback Edition
© Copyright 2019 Linell Jeppsen

Wolfpack Publishing
6032 Wheat Penny Avenue
Las Vegas, NV 89122

wolfpackpublishing.com

Paperback ISBN 978-1-64119-509-6
eBook ISBN 978-1-62918-602-3

DEADMAN'S LAMENT

PART I

Coming over a high hill, twelve-year-old Matthew Wilcox searched the far green slopes for Adeline, his father's mare. Addie liked to wander but now, ever since they sold her yearling colt to old man Hensley, she had taken to chasin' north. It was Mattie's duty to fetch that mare home. Spotting a flash of white by the Pinckney trail, he shook his head. The horse stood at the barbed wire fence, pawing at the ground, calling her offspring back home. *Shoot*, he thought, *she's as lonely as a teetotaler in a saloon.*

Mattie grinned, feeling proud that he remembered one of his father's sayings so exact. But his smile faltered and died when he recalled that his pa, Robert Wilcox, had not yet returned from his last trip into town. It was only Monday, though, so no call to get in a ruffle.

He clicked his tongue, "Come on, Pete. Let's go and grab that old jug-headed hoss."

Pete, the mule, farted in reply. Looping the lead rope around Pete's neck, Mattie moved ahead on foot, keeping a sharp eye on the rocky ground that sheltered timber rattlers and skinny rabbits.

Pete was never afraid of any old snake but those jackrabbits did him in every time. He would get to shuddering and twitching and, next thing you knew, that mule would be running as fast as greased lightning or he'd go rodeo. Last time that happened, Mattie could barely sit down for a week, his tailbone was so bruised and sore.

Stepping carefully, they wound down the switch-back trail, landing in the valley below. He stuck two fingers in his mouth and whistled. The mare left off crying for her foal long enough to turn and look at the approaching boy. Pete brayed in reproach and lowered his lips to the tender grass at his hooves.

Mattie pulled the lead from around the mule's neck, muttering, "Come on, Pete. Let's go…"

Pete flapped his long ears and hunkered down, calf-kneed…a sure sign that he wasn't going anywhere, at least until he had his fill of sweet grass. The boy sighed and let the rope drop. At most, the mare was only a quarter mile away, so he grabbed the hackamore and took off walking.

Although the wind pinched with icy fingers, the sun was warm. Mattie took off his felt hat and stuck it in his belt. The breeze ruffled his hair and tears streamed from his eyes. Bending over, he grabbed a stout stick and swished at the grass and wildflowers in his path.

He thought about the harsh words his folks had whispered Friday night as he and his little sister Maude eavesdropped from the loft. Mattie wasn't sure why his mother was so mad but it had to do with his daddy, and no money to spare. Yet it seemed to him that, every time his pa went to town, things were better rather than worse. After all, Pa had brought Pete, the mule, home a year ago and, one time, he brought home the new danger-wire and two ready-made dresses, one each for Ma and Maude.

Now, though, his ma was madder than a wet hen and his pa was late getting home. Calculating the distance to town while he lopped the tops off the dandelions at his feet, Mattie wondered. Pa's gelding, Joe, could keep a brisk trot going for miles on end. It was thirty miles to the fort, so Pa could make it into town with daylight to spare. He had left on Saturday… even if Pa had lingered through Sunday to shop for supplies, he should be home by now.

He glanced up at the sudden pall in the sky. The sun hid behind a large black cloud and tiny beads of frozen rain were suspended between earth and sky. Mattie shivered at the chill. The mare had stopped pacing and stood waiting for his approach. She was sweated, her mane speckled with ice.

"Come on, Sis…," Mattie crooned as he walked up slow. "Let's go on home."

The horse complied, bending her muzzle to nibble the weeds growing alongside the road. He smoothed the hackamore up the mare's nose and over her ears.

He took a double fistful of her mane, jumped up bare-back, and ambled toward the mule grazing at the far end of the valley.

Mattie started to eat one of the bacon sandwiches his ma had made for his lunch when, suddenly, Pete lurched to the left and—with a panicked bray—jumped backwards. Glaring through the fitful sunlight, he saw a small pack of wolves worrying at Pete's flanks.

"Haw!" Mattie cried, kicking the mare hard. Addie took off running with a startled snort. It only took a couple of minutes to reach the trembling mule. The wolves had run off at his approach but he saw them gather at the foot of a rocky crag bordering the valley's northern rim.

The pack stared down at him with cool appraisal and the boy felt a tingle of fear. It was unusual at this time of year for wolves to attack in the bright of day and even more uncommon to go after as formidable a beast as a full-grown mule with a human so close by. Studying the wolves' slat-ribbed bodies and hollow eyes, Mattie understood that they were starving to death and had thrown caution to the wind in their quest for sustenance.

Both horse and mule were skittish and blowing hard with fear. Although his hands were clammy with sweat, he reached for his slingshot. Taking careful aim, he shot a rock at the lead wolf, a big rangy male with a gray muzzle. His rock fell short but ricocheted upward, hitting it in the belly. The animal spun in mid-air with a yelp and the pack took off over the hill and out of sight.

Shaking and too scared to climb down off the horse's back, Mattie bent down to see what damage, if any, the wolves had done to the mule. There were two rake marks across Pete's rump, but little blood and he seemed sound. The boy gathered up the lead rope and, clicking his teeth, sharply brought the two animals to a trot. His blood was still racing and he cursed himself for being a coward.

He decided to cut back and take the road home instead of going overland. Common sense told him the wolves were long gone by now but the idea of following hard on their tail did not appeal. He slowed Addie and rode a wide circle back toward the road. A couple of times, he turned around to study the landscape, making sure the wolves were not tracking and then sighed with self-disgust; going back on the road would cost him a couple of hours and make his ma worry.

Mattie was about a hundred yards from the road when he heard a distant shout. Pulling the mare up short, he sat and watched as a draft horse hove into view, followed by a large wagon. A horse and its rider walked along beside them. The wagon driver was speaking to the solitary rider but stopped talking and pointed in Mattie's direction.

"Hey boy, how far to the Wilcox farm?" the rider called.

"Well," Mattie hesitated. "You're on it...the south end of it, anyway."

The man on the horse spoke to the driver for a moment and then he spurred up and trotted toward Mattie. The rider sat high in the saddle and wore a wealth of silver on his saddle leather and on his person. The boy saw a star on the man's chest and realized it was the sheriff approaching. He slid off the mare's back and waited.

The sheriff creaked to a stop in front of him. The huge bay gelding bared its teeth at Pete, pissing a heavy stream on the grass in front of where Mattie stood.

"Dang it," the man muttered and climbed down off his horse. Leading the gelding away a bit, he hobbled it and walked back, hitching his belt leather and swatting his hat at a persistent fly. He was a heavy-set man of middle years with thinning ginger hair and the red nose of a serious drinker. His eyes were fixed on Mattie's face and something within his gaze made the boy's heart race with fear.

"My name is Bradley...Sheriff Bradley. Are you Robert Wilcox's boy?"

Mattie nodded and said, "Yessir. My name is Matthew, sir."

The sheriff clutched his hat in both hands and growled, "Well, Matthew...I got a piece of bad news for you, sorry to say."

Mattie glanced at the wagon on the road and the driver who leaned against it chewing a piece of cheat grass. Suddenly understanding, Mattie started to run in that direction but the sheriff leaned down and grabbed his arm.

"Whoa, son. Why don't we sit for a spell afore you go runnin' off? That's your pa, for sure, but the doc's got him all fixed up proper for buryin'."

Mattie felt dizzy and his ears rang. Looking up at the fat, old sheriff from where he sat on the ground, Mattie realized he must have fainted. The man was kneeling over him with a canteen, urging him to drink. Mattie shook his head and dashed tears from his face.

"What happened?" he cried. "Did someone hurt him?"

"Well, no. Your pa had a stroke." Bradley scratched at the stubble on his chin. "Thing is, though," he continued, "Doc thinks yer pa had a stroke on account of what happened." The sheriff sighed.

"What do you mean? What happened before that?" Mattie felt tears running down his face but could not make them stop.

"Well...and this is gonna be hard on you and yer family, you understand, but yer pa put this farm up on the poker table."

"What do you mean?" Mattie cried. "My pa doesn't gamble!"

The sheriff nodded. "I know, son. Doc Wilcox was not known for it, but he played Sunday night, that's for sure." He shrugged his shoulders and shook his head. "From what I hear, he was doing real good too, but the stakes got too high and his luck jus' ran out."

Knees popping, the sheriff stood up, reaching his

hand down to the boy. "This story is best told once, son. I aim to have you ride with me back home to your ma, alright?"

Ignoring the sheriff's help, Mattie climbed to his feet. Grabbing Addie's reins, he started walking toward the wagon. The driver tipped his hat and climbed aboard while he tied the mare to the back. Bradley tied Pete to the opposite side while Mattie climbed in next to his pa's body. The doctor had wrapped Robert Wilcox in an old horse blanket. A note pinned on the blanket read, *Propertee of Stokes Livery.*

Mattie saw that his father's blond hair stuck out from the top of the covering. It seemed improper, somehow, and not knowing what else to do, he pulled his hat from his belt and placed it on his pa's head. It was too small, of course, but it made Mattie feel better.

The wagon lurched toward home while Mattie Wilcox rode guard and the sheriff contemplated the sorry task that lay ahead.

By the time they pulled up in front of the Wilcox's house it was late afternoon. There had been no conversing along the way except for the occasional comment on the early onset of winter or muttered curses toward the balky lead horse.

Mattie had fallen asleep for a while and dreamt of

his home...the only home he had ever known. It was a fine place...chinked logs and a sturdy roof that only leaked once in a while, usually after a sudden, spring thaw. He dreamed of Christmas' past and how his pa would swing through the front door, sometimes with presents in his arms for his "womenfolk."

Waking with a start, he recalled how his pa would lift him up onto his shoulders and say, "You are the king, my boy...the king of all you see!"

Mattie and his sister had learned long ago that his ma and pa came from West Virginia. Sarah Cummings, Mattie's mother, was from a family of well-to-do landowners; Robert Wilcox was the son of a prosperous attorney.

Robert was well educated, whimsical and completely in love with the notion of settling in the new western territories. Abandoning his father's law office, Robert packed up his new bride—incurring the wrath of Sarah's family—and joined a wagon train heading to the Northwest into the exotic new land of Columbia, which would later, be re-named Washington State.

He had no real understanding of how hard the overland trek would be on his young wife though. Whereas the journey was a wonderful adventure for Robert, it was a terror-filled and dreadful ordeal for Sarah. Robert's original plan was to set up office in the booming new city of Seattle. By the time they reached the Spokane area though, his beautiful Sarah was so undone by nerves and illness, Robert feared he would lose her entirely. The young couple abandoned the wagon train in Spokane and settled into their new lives.

Within the year, Robert purchased land thirty miles away from Fort Colville...a hundred acres of pasture ringed by high mountains. It was rich in timber, water and wild game. With the help of two out-of-work cowboys and one old Indian named Joseph Two-Toes, Robert built a fine house and barn. A year later, Matthew was born, followed by Maude.

The children led a charmed life. For years, Robert rode into town and stayed there for a week at a time, taking care of the sundry land disputes and criminal cases that came along. There was still money left in Sarah's dowry that the family dipped into upon occasion. Although Robert's payments often came in the form of chickens, or eggs or canned goods, the family prospered.

At least at first- then lack of money finally took a toll on Sarah's nerves. She had been raised in wealthy splendor and she was unable to hide her disappointment with their present circumstances. Robert seemed unwilling or unable to demand cash for services rendered and the more she pushed for extra money the more Robert fled her constant nagging until, finally, his one week in town turned into two, or even three weeks gone. When he finally found his way back home, he stayed as far away from her as possible.

When they did spend time together, furious, whispered quarrels erupted over nothing and a tension-filled silence fell upon the once happy household. Soon, the Wilcox children understood that their parents' love was dying. The last time his pa left, Sarah stood in the open doorway of their home with tears trickling, unheeded, down her pale cheeks.

Mattie took her hand in his and asked, "What's the matter, Ma?"

She shook her head once, whispering, "He's gone… and he might as well stay gone for all the good he does."

Mattie was shocked." Ma! Why would you say such a thing?" She turned away, saying nothing.

Mattie winced now, remembering the anger in her eyes. He sat up from where he had fallen asleep, nestled at his dead father's side and peered over the edge of the tall-sided wagon.

His ma stood on the front porch, Maude by her side. Sarah Wilcox met her son's eyes as they pulled up in front of the house and Mattie knew that he would never forget the look of guilty sorrow in his ma's eyes, even if he lived to be a hundred years old.

SICK AT HEART

MATTHEW STARED OUT AT THE FALLING SNOW. THE BAD weather had started two days before, freezing the rutted roads and coating the mud puddles with a solid scrim of ice. He heard a distant shout and peered through the dirty glass at the smithy's lean-to across the street. He could see the glow of the blacksmith's fires reflecting off the walls. He shivered at the chill that pervaded the small shack he and his family lived in.

After Robert died, the family was granted two months to clear out of their home. Sarah Wilcox had telegraphed the news of Robert's demise and the change of circumstances to her people back home in Virginia but, so far, no reply was forthcoming.

Joseph Two-Toes came to help them pack up and move, though there wasn't much to bother with. Sheriff Bradley and two of his deputies stood guard while Mattie, Maude and Sarah scurried back and forth from the house to the wagon with personal items tucked into trunks, satchels, and flour sacks. Richard Child—the man who had won the farm from Robert Wilcox—sat on his horse. Along with his father and two brothers, they watched suspiciously and kept a running tally of every item carried from the house.

Mattie loathed the men with every fiber of his being. The sheriff, although sympathetic to the family's plight, made sure to point out that the deal was fair and square, witnessed and bound by law. Mattie understood but still couldn't tolerate the smug satisfaction on Child's face, or the way the man's brother spat in Joseph's direction every time the Indian passed by.

Sarah was devastated by grief and shame. However, some semblance of her wealthy Southern upbringing rose to the surface that day. As she walked by Child with the last of her personal belongings, she held her head high. Wrinkling her nose slightly, as though affronted by an unpleasant odor, Sarah Wilcox managed to make the interlopers look away in embarrassment.

Little Maude was the only one who turned around to look at the homestead as they drove down the dirt road toward town. Mattie stared straight ahead, eyes glazed with tears, his cheeks burning with humiliation. Sarah pulled her shawl up over her head, closed her eyes and went to sleep. Their new life had begun.

The only house available they could afford was a ramshackle hut at the far edge of Pinkington, close to the railroad track and a whorehouse. There were actually three brothels in town. Two snugged up next to the fort and were filled with healthy young girls, high quality liquor, and the services of the town's best doctor. The whores next to Mattie's new home, though, were not so fortunate. Many of them were well past their prime and in ill health. Their cheap perfumes could not compete with the smell of the livery and the slaughterhouses on that end of town. Yet the women were kind enough and, on occasion, offered help and comfort.

Mattie went over every morning to sweep, bring in firewood, and haul in hot water for the women's weekly baths. At first, they teased him over his fine manners and educated tongue. Later—realizing that Mattie actually knew his alphabet—the whores asked him to read passages from the Bible or decipher the occasional newspaper article or letter that came their way. There were only a pitiful few of those, however.

Mattie glanced toward the back corner of the room where his mother lay sleeping, facing the wall, and he could hear her soft snores. He saw the bottle of laudanum by the bed and shook his head in dismay. It was over half empty already and the doctor had been by just yesterday. What little money they had left was quickly lining the sawbones's pocket and Mattie needed a dollar for the headmistress or Maude could not continue her education at school.

He decided to run over to the livery later and see if old man, Stokes could use a hand with bucking bales or rubbing down the animals. If nothing else, he might get to pet Addie a little and give her the broken carrot he had found in the rubbish pile.

Addie and Joe, his father's gelding, had gone to the livery to be sold for food, medicine and rent. The family still owned Pete but, as Stokes was fond of saying, "Hay don't come cheap," any proceeds from the sale of the horses would go against the cost of feeding the mule.

Mattie was putting on his coat when there was a light scratch at the door. He turned around in surprise; no one ever came to call. It was as though the proper folks in town thought that misfortune was catching, like the flu. For all that Mattie knew, maybe it was.

He walked to the door and opened it to find Joseph Two-Toes and his little granddaughter, Tawnee, standing on the stoop. The old man looked near frozen to death and his shabby old blanket was speckled with ice. Little Tawnee stared up at Mattie with haunted eyes.

"Joseph...Sir, please come in," Mattie stuttered, stepping away from the door.

The tiny cook-stove was blazing hot but the house was so flimsy all the heat escaped out the roof or through the crooked seams in the exterior walls. Judging by the way his guests looked though, Matthew did not think that it was likely they would complain much over the shabby hospitality.

"Can I get you some coffee, sir?" Mattie asked anxiously.

For a moment, it looked as though Joseph was

going to fall right over and his granddaughter looked almost as bad. The last time Mattie had seen the little girl she was laughing and chasing Maude around with a dandelion, intent on rubbing butter on her opponent's face. Now Mattie could see that her olive complexion was gray and her huge brown eyes were hollow with fatigue.

Joseph held up a hand and asked, "You got work, Matew? I must earn money to buy food and medicine for my daughter's daughter."

Mattie shook his head. "I'm sorry, sir. There's not a lot of work around here...not at this time of year, anyway. My ma and I can give you some food, though. We would be happy to do that."

Joseph stared at Mattie with hooded eyes while snow melted from the blanket on his shoulders, speckling the floor underneath his chair like tear tracks. He shook his head.

"No...no gifts. Joseph Two-Toes will work for food."

Mattie sighed. There was no work to be had. If there were, he would be doing it instead of worrying over how to pay the bills. He smiled at the old Indian and said, "Okay, sir. I will find you some work. In the meanwhile, why don't we get you something to eat?"

Matthew grabbed the cook-pot, filled it with water and some oats for porridge. He cut a wrinkled apple into slices and asked Joseph for news while he added the fruit to the mixture.

Joseph chewed his upper lip as he thought about

what to say to the boy. Matthew Wilcox was a good child but Joseph's news might not be what he wanted, or needed, to hear. Still, now that Robert was dead, maybe the boy needed to hear the truth whether he liked it or not. He was chief in his family now and needed to know the weather, for good or ill.

"My people still fight. They fight against the black cloaks and the white settlers. They fight one another." The old man sighed. "They are very angry, I think."

"Also, I hear that the fort is going to shut down." Joseph shrugged at the expression in the boy's eyes. "But I could be wrong."

Mattie set a plate of bread and some peach preserves on the table in front of the little girl but she made no move to eat. Instead, she closed her eyes as though the very sight of food caused her pain.

"Come on, Tawnee. Have something to eat," Mattie coaxed, frowning in consternation when she turned away. In the fitful firelight, her face suddenly took on the aspect of a human skull like the one Doc Abrams had in his little office by the hotel.

"You're tired, I reckon," he said, adding, "Let's get you bedded down here where it's warm."

Mattie grabbed a quilt off a shelf and made a pallet on the floor by the wood stove. Joseph stood up slowly and laid the girl on the quilt; she turned over and put her thumb in her mouth.

"She's tired, isn't she, sir?" Mattie looked toward the older man and saw that Joseph had taken a long step backward and now leaned up against the wall. His skin was the color of milk gone bad and his eyes rolled back in his head like a loco horse.

Mattie felt a thrill of fear, realizing suddenly that Joseph and his granddaughter were not just tired, but ill. Terribly ill, judging the way the old man stood wheezing and trembling.

"What have you done?" Sarah's harsh whisper filled the room.

Mattie whirled around and stared at his mother. She stood in the doorway, glaring at him through drug-crazed eyes. Mattie remembered, too late, that his ma held a deep-seated fear and hatred of Indians. She had seen the tail end of too many unfortunate incidents on her overland journey. Now that Robert was gone, she was not afraid to say how much she despised the red men.

"Those Injuns have the pox, Matthew, and you brought them inside! Now we're all going to die!" Sarah abruptly broke into a fit of giggles and did a little jig.

Mattie stared in horror as his mother danced in the doorway and Joseph Two-Toes did his best to stay upright. His heart was tapping against his rib cage like a trapped bird. Ma was right, of course, but there was no call to be mean.

Suddenly angry, he barked, "Ma! You go back to bed now! I'll call you if I need you."

Sarah Wilcox swayed in place, her momentary clarity of purpose gone as soon as it had come, like a will o' the wisp in a turbulent wind. She stepped into the other room, lay back down in her bed and turned her face away.

Matthew gazed at Joseph and, for a moment, wanted to shoot him dead. Why did that damn old Indian have to come here anyway? Didn't his family have enough trouble already? He hesitated for a moment and then ran to help Joseph slide down onto the floor.

Two days later, Mattie and Doc Abrams were the only ones left alive in the house. Maude had been taken away (for her own safety) to an orphanage in Spokane. Joseph Two-Toes had died that morning; Sarah Wilcox and the little girl named Tawnee had passed the day before.

Mattie's eyes were hot and red from fatigue and unshed tears. He expected to fall ill any second. In fact, the doctor kept checking his eyes, throat and brow for signs of smallpox. Finally, the doctor set his cold coffee down with a sigh.

"I don't think you got it," he said. "But, in truth, it don't matter much. The people here ain't gonna let you stick around anyway." He rubbed a shaking hand over his eyes.

"People get spooked when it comes to the pox... superstitious. I could holler out on the street corner that Matthew Wilcox ain't infected but still they would take off a runnin', see?"

Mattie sat in his chair and stared at the old doctor. He had almost hated the man for giving his ma the medicine that rendered her useless to the family who needed her. He did not like the way the doctor smelled, like dirty laundry and hooch. Moreover, he didn't like the way Abrams looked, with his one wandering eye and his yellow, gap-toothed grin.

Mattie knew, though, that he had gained a sort of wisdom about people in the last couple of days... and who they were on the inside. Doc Abrams had worked valiantly to save Joseph Two-Toes and his grand-daughter despite the fact they were Indians. He had eased his mother's passing with as much kindness and dignity as was possible and had given freely of his medicine without ever mentioning how dear it was. He was a good man.

A NEW BEGINNING

It was late March. Crows cackled from the birch trees and buttercups cast the sun's reflection off the water's lazy swell. Mattie was hunched up against a pile of moldy ropes, gnawing on a piece of jerked venison. He was basking in the early morning sunlight, marveling at the fact that he was finally content. It felt as if he had survived a terrible storm; a dense, foggy miasma of sorrow, fear and doubt. But now, the spring thaw was melting the frozen dam his heart had become.

He stared across the sun-spangled water and heard the Indians who fished on the far shore laughing, exchanging raunchy jokes and issuing challenges to one another. Their strange pointed nets glistened with salmon and trout and their fires were banked low for the drying racks.

Occasionally, Mattie was allowed to help. For some reason, the Indians found his company appealing.

Maybe it was the solemn wisdom in his green eyes, or the respect they sensed in his demeanor that permitted a white boy into their sacred conclave.

No matter, there would be no fishing today. Agents from the Northwest Trading Company were expected sometime later in the afternoon. Mattie didn't like the company agents. They acted as if every pelt in the Northwest Territories belonged to them exclusively, as though granted to them by God above.

Every time one of them visited the outpost, Jacques Dupre' would sulk for days afterward. Whether a suited money agent or a stinking trapper, they ended up insulting Jacques, Mattie, or a member of Dupre's family either by a word, a whispered insult, or a lewd glance.

When Doc Abrams first dropped Mattie off at the outpost four months earlier, the boy feared the worst. Many trading posts were little more than flea-infested, ramshackle huts. He was pleasantly surprised, however, to find a clean and neatly patched canvas tent snugged up next to a tiny, two-story frame house. The tent held hides and hanging slabs of beef, elk, venison and pork. Tidy barrels contained salt, pickles, meal and tallow. Every implement needed for farming, trapping or building hung from the walls and ceiling. It was clean as a Catholic virgin- as Jacques was fond of saying.

There was a small stable with four stalls, a smithy and a round pen; now the only occupant in the stable was Pete. Surprisingly, Abrams had shown up a couple of weeks before with the mule hitched to the back of his wagon.

"That dang old miser, Stokes has got enough straw outta you, I reckon," Abrams grumbled when he handed the lead rope to Mattie along with a small sack of coins.

"That bit of cash is for your pa's horses," he added. "Shoulda got more for 'em than I did, but he plum tuckered me out with his bartering."

Smiling, Abrams put a hand on Mattie's shoulder. "There's about eighteen dollars there, son. Put that by and save what you earn. Won't be long and you can go fetch your sister… maybe take a train back to your people in Virginny."

Overwhelmed, Mattie threw his arms around the old doctor in a spontaneous hug. Suddenly, they were interrupted.

"Matthew! Damn, Minette, where is that boy?"

When Mattie first arrived at the trading post, he was terrified of the little Frenchman. Jacque was short but wide with wild black hair that seemed to sprout from every orifice like porcupine quills. His eyebrows met in the middle of his forehead and wiggled like an agitated caterpillar. Jacques never spoke when he could holler and his heavy French accent was so slurred and vowel-laden, Mattie could barely understand a word he said.

It only took a couple of days, though, to understand that Mr. Dupre' was a kind and generous employer who adored his wife, Minette, and their only child,

Marie. For all his bluster, the Frenchman seemed in awe of his diminutive spouse who ran the house with military zeal. Her floors were scrubbed on a daily basis and her one glass window gleamed fiercely.

When Doc Abrams and Mattie first entered the Dupre' home, Minette took one look at the frightened, hollow-cheeked boy and wrapped him in her arms. "Ah, Jacques," she cried. "Thees boy ees starved and so sad, no?" The tiny woman sat him in one of the kitchen chairs.

"You sit here now and eat...yes?" she continued as she scooped stew into a bowl, placing bread and fresh cream butter on the table. Minette scurried around the kitchen scolding, laughing and cleaning while Mattie ate and the men talked quietly in the front parlor.

Although he could only understand one word in three the little woman uttered, it didn't matter. Mattie knew he had found safe harbor in the Dupre' family's outpost. In addition, he couldn't take his eyes off the young girl who sat sewing in the far corner by the stove.

Back before the trouble began with his father's death and the family's unfortunate change of situation, there were—on occasion—visitors to the farm. Sarah had never forgotten how to entertain and once every few months she would invite the finest families in town for a soiree.

In that time, Mattie met many a fine miss. Some were haughty beyond belief, and some were sweet. Many were bored and naughty with it. None of them though—with their fancy clothes and starchy curls—could compare to the beautiful girl who sat and gazed at him from under her eyelashes.

She had her mother's fine, pale complexion and petite size, but her hair was like her father's, black as night and aloft with curls. She had her father's bright blue eyes as well. Those eyes stared at him and left him tongue-tied and hot under the collar.

Over the next few months, Mattie and Marie became the best of friends. They did most of their many chores together. When they had time to spare, the children sometimes fished on the river's banks or helped the Indians haul in their nets. The native children laughingly called them skunk children because the girl was so dark and the boy so bright with his golden hair and light green eyes.

Mattie was too young yet to feel much in the way of sexual tension but, occasionally after a long day of chores, he would lie awake at night thinking of Marie. He loved the way she spoke and her tinkling laughter; he admired her strength, both mental and physical, and the tender way she dealt with animals. He loved her soft hair…her sweet breath. He loved her, period.

He finally decided to ask for her hand in marriage when he was old enough. He figured that day would come when he turned sixteen. Meanwhile, he needed to earn his stripes with Papa Jacques, which wasn't too difficult. He only needed to work hard and keep a cheery, respectful tongue in his mouth.

Jumping up, Mattie wiped greasy hands on his

pants and walked into the barn. He scrambled up the ladder to the loft and started tossing hay down to Pete and into the other three stalls. Chances were the agents would stay the night and that meant housing their live-stock as well. Suddenly, he heard a great thunder of hooves in the distance, approaching fast.

Stepping outside, he peered up the trailhead. The Pinckney road was some fifty yards or so from the outpost and it was prudent, if not simply polite, to go slowly on the steep, winding path that led to the build-ings and the beach beyond. Mattie was shocked when the sound of shots rang out and he heard Mr. Dupre' shout for his wife and daughter to run and hide.

For a split second, Mattie wondered if he should hide as well. Then he decided to go help Minette and Marie. That moment of hesitation saved his life. Running toward the front stoop, Mattie saw a horse careen around the corner of the building. He took one look at the horse's rider and dove under the porch. The man wore malevolence on his brow like a dark hat and the smile that split his face spoke volumes about his intentions.

Mattie watched as five more horses and a couple of mules crowded in behind the leader. He knew, instinc-tively, that this was trouble on the hoof. The men on horseback were filthy and leering as they studied the tent and house beside it. The leader wore black oilskin and his teeth were very white against his unkempt, salt-and-pepper beard. He spurred his foaming mare so she reared up, screaming.

"Hello, the house!" he called. His voice was girlish, in sharp contrast to his size and demeanor. He was grinning and the riders who accompanied him cheered and hooted in excitement.

There was no response from within and the man's grin faded. "Y'all need to come out now. Come on out or we will fire you out! You hear me, Frenchie?"

Mattie winced. Somehow these bad men knew about the Dupre' outpost and that, on occasion, Jacques held the army payroll and heavy bags of silver the Northwest Trading Company paid for the pelts brought in from the high mountain trappers.

This was not one of those times though or, at least, not yet. The pelts were bundled up and ready to go but the agents hadn't arrived to pick them up. *These bandits have poor timing*, Mattie thought. Not that it would matter to rogues like these; they wouldn't believe Dupre' even if they bothered to ask.

Mattie stared down the forested slope toward the Indians that fished the river's shore and despaired. They were too far away to see the trading post through the tall trees. Mattie also knew that the Indians disliked getting involved in "white man's business".

The leader of the gang studied the house and its attached tent with eyes as cold and gray as frosted water. He lifted his upper lip and spat, letting a long, yellow string of chew drizzle from between his two front teeth.

"Top Hat … Daryl, go in and fetch that fuckin' Frenchie. Grab the payroll while you're at it."

Mattie's blood ran cold. Dupre' almost never let Minette or Marie mingle with the customers. Some of them were downright mean and others were as wild and feral as the beasts they hunted. Still others were so starved for the love of a woman they blushed and panted in almost uncontrollable lust while in mixed company.

The only customers Jacques allowed in his kitchen were trading company agents; not because he liked or trusted Northwest Traders more, but because a good percentage of Dupre's income came from the handling of furs. Mattie suddenly realized that the leader of these outlaws must have been in or around the house on company business and was now double-dealing.

The two men started moving toward the house. One was tall and stick-thin, with dull eyes and long, bucked teeth like a rat; the other was so fat that rolls of flesh oozed out from under his belt and his many chins jiggled when he stepped onto the porch.

Mattie felt around and pulled his slingshot from his pants pocket. He thought, for sure, that the women would be all right; they were hidden in a dugout beneath an ancient Tamarack just beyond the outhouse. Mattie worried more for Mr. Dupre'. Although Jacques was a good, kind man, he was possessed of a fiery temper and was a bad shot with a rifle.

The two outlaws walked across the porch and Mattie held his nose as dust sifted down on his head and shoulders. The door was bolted shut but the wood was old and gave away with one swift kick. Almost immediately, Mattie heard rifle fire.

"Gawd damint!" one of the men exclaimed. "That Frenchie almost took my dang head off!"

Mattie heard the other man laugh. "That's what ya get fer makin' yourself such a fat target. Now look sharp! That varmint is around here somewhere."

Mattie started to edge away to the far side of the porch. He thought he might be able to sneak around the east side of the house and fetch the womenfolk away to safety while the others were distracted. Keeping one eye on the leader of the gang, he scooted backward in the dirt. Seeing the sun's rays near the end of the structure, Mattie was just about to scramble out into the open when a large, rough hand seized his shoulder. He couldn't help but squeal in fright as he was lifted into the air.

"Lookie what I found, Boss!"

Although Mattie struggled and fought with all his might, he could not break free of the hands that held him by the scruff of the neck like a puppy. Twisting around in mid-air, he stared at his captor in shock. The man was enormous with shiny, dark skin and wild, kinky hair. He wore plaid pants that rode high above his ankles but he was bare-chested. Scars crossed his torso and shoulders, his dull black eyes smoldering with dull hatred.

The boss nodded and said, "Very fine catch, Tulu... extra rations for you tonight."

Tulu bowed his head. "Yes, Boss. Thank you, Boss. What do I do with this critter?"

The leader studied Mattie's trembling body for a moment. His eyes were a brilliant blue and, although he seemed to be in his mid to late 50s, Mattie could tell that he had once been a fine-looking man...*a cool drink of water on a hot summer's day*, as his daddy used to say.

Now, though, time and trouble had etched the man's face with scowl marks and deep brackets around thin, downturned lips. Those same lips turned up in a grin and he said, "Tie him to the mule. He's comin' with us."

"Yes, Suh." Tulu answered. Despite Mattie's howls of protest, the boy soon found himself trussed as tightly as a hog, face down on a stinking horse blanket on back of a mule.

A few moments later, there was another round of gunfire and a hoarse shout of pain from inside the house. Mattie turned his head and watched as the two bandits hauled Jacques Dupre's limp body out into the front yard. They dumped him face down on the ground at the leader's feet, kicking him over so that his dead eyes stared up into the sky.

Then, the man named Top Hat held up a leather sack. "Found this, Randall, with about twenty silver dollars inside. Didn't find no payroll, though, sorry to say."

Randall Penny considered the small sack in his cousin's hand and cursed. He had heard that the trading company boys were headed down here today but they must not have come by yet which meant the shed was probably rich with furs. Problem was, their wagons were over twenty miles away and, even on horseback, there was no possible way to get the wagons back here in time to load up those furs without being caught by either the company boys or the law.

"Shit-fire," he muttered, scratching at his beard. Then he grinned and said, "Top Hat, you and Daryl go on around back by that big Tam. There is a trap door just east of the tree. There you will find a hideout. Go and fetch the womenfolk out here."

Mattie had watched as his friend and protector, Dupre', was dumped at Randall's feet like a dead dog. Tears of sorrow filled his eyes and wet the blanket on which he lay. He had thought—hoped—that Marie and her mother were safe. Now he knew that the young girl he had fallen in love with and planned to marry was doomed.

"NO!" he howled in anguish.

A flock of crows lifted as one, staining the sky over-head with inky shadows before dispersing and flying north. The Indians who fished the far shore of the river shuddered and looked away from the sudden, ill omen that darkened their day.

4

A CROW'S CRY

"Tulu! Shut that boy up!" Randall snapped.

Instantly, Tulu's large hand covered Mattie's cries. "You hush now afore I eats you for dinner!" he growled.

Mattie wanted to scream even louder but the man's hand was so big it covered both his mouth and his nose. Suddenly, Mattie found himself unable to breathe and he whipped his head from side to side in search of air. The hand tightened and Mattie understood that he would suffocate if he didn't stop struggling; he quieted and lay back down on the woven blanket.

Tulu stared at him for a moment and asked, "You be quiet now, boy?"

Mattie nodded mutely and sighed when the Negro tied a dirty bandana around his mouth as a gag. "There now. You be good and Tulu don't eat you...or worse, Boss don't give you to his cousin, Top Hat."

Mattie looked up into Tulu's face and thought he

saw something. A flash of kindness maybe or the warmth of fear in the man's dark eyes. He started to speak but Tulu shook his head and walked away.

Mattie heard a shout in the distance and his heart sank. It was Marie's mother, Minette, screeching in outrage. Then the two men came around the corner of the house. Daryl was dragging her by one arm while Top Hat carried Marie over his shoulder like a sack of beans. Minette started to scream in earnest when she saw her husband sprawled in the dirt in front of Randall's horse.

Mattie saw Marie struggle fiercely but he realized that her wrists were bound with a short piece of rope. Top Hat dumped the young girl on the ground close to her dead father and she crawled, weeping, toward his body. Minette threw her head back and let out a wail of sorrow so profound even Randall looked away.

Sagging to the ground in grief, Minette crept to her husband's side. While mother and daughter wept bitter tears, the outlaws huddled together, deciding what to do.

Mattie couldn't quite hear what they were saying but, suddenly, Top Hat stepped back, pulled his pistol and shot Minette in the back. Mattie groaned behind his gag and tears clogged his throat. Marie sat up in shock, staring at the woman who had given birth to her now lying prostrate on her husband's chest. Minette was not dead though...not yet. She whispered something to her daughter who leaned down listening intently to her words. Then she was gone and Marie looked up at the man who had shot her parents for twenty pieces of silver. Her blue eyes were wide with shock and her lips were twisted in a parody of a smile that sent chills through Mattie's heart.

The girl who stared at the road agents with a death's head grin and vacant eyes was no longer the girl he had fallen in love with, Mattie knew. Her heart had just been ripped out and torn to pieces while he watched, trussed up like a piece of meat, unable to help. He hung his head in shame and sorrow and waited for the bullet that never came.

"Put her on the other mule," Randall muttered.

Mattie looked up in surprise. He was sure that Marie would be murdered, too. Instead, she was going to be held captive along with him. He felt his heart swell with hope. Some of his father's sayings swirled around in Mattie's head like a flock of birds. *Where there is life, there is hope* and *Where there is a will, there is a way.*

Tulu strode over to a mule that was harnessed close to the animal Mattie was tied on. The big man held Marie gently enough but it didn't seem to matter much to the girl one way or the other. Her eyes were blank with incomprehension and, although Mattie's gaze met hers as Tulu tied her to the restless mule, there was no recognition in those blue depths.

Randall, who had not dismounted while his henchmen laid waste to their world, rode close to Mattie and said, "That little gash will fetch a handsome price at a place I know of in Seattle."

He studied the look of rage and revulsion that filled Mattie's eyes and added, "Don't you be getting any funny ideas in that pretty head of yours. You will stay with us for a while. We've been in need of a hand in this outfit and I think you will do jus' fine."

He spurred his horse, simultaneously pulling the reins back so the mare squealed in pain and reared up, pawing the air.

"If you do a good job, we'll take care of you. If not, I'll gut you like a fish and feed you to my nigger."

They rode hard then, for hours and hours, west into the setting sun. Sometime in the late afternoon, the band of outlaws rode into a crevasse. Mattie stared at the tall rock formation in awe. The setting sun reached long, yellow fingers into the shadowy tunnel and illuminated glittering veins of silver and gold running like sparkly ribbons through the granite walls. He wondered if those golden specks were "real" or the fabled "Fool's Gold" he had heard tales of in the past.

He looked over at Marie and saw that she was asleep; her cheeks were flushed and her long, black lashes fanned across them like a bird's feathers.

The horse's hooves sounded like rolling thunder as they emerged from the tunnel. Milling around in the cool evening's dusk, Mattie saw a campfire across an expanse of pasture; its orange reflection made the distant cliffs look like hell's fire.

He shuddered in fear as he saw the silhouette of many more men in the fire's glow. Looking up, he saw an evening star twinkling distantly in a purple sky, and he felt as lost and lonely as that star. Even as he watched, the star was snuffed out, obscured by a cloud or the slant of the Earth's horizon.

Then the mule stepped forward with a jolt and they were galloping toward the firelight and whatever evil surrounded it. The band of highwaymen rode into the encampment with shouts of glee. Mattie saw that about a dozen or so men surrounded the fire. An Indian ran up and took the reins of Randall's horse while he got down out of the saddle. Two more men ambled over and took the reins of Top Hat and Daryl's horses while the rest came and stared at where he and Marie sat tied to the mules.

"Whatcher got there, Boss?" A middle-aged man with loose, tobacco-stained lips stood close to Marie and ogled the young girl. He seemed to be simple-minded but Mattie saw that he was rubbing at his crotch with unabashed attention.

"You leave off staring at that girl, Rooster!" Randall snarled and the man took a stumbling step backward; the other men stepped away as well.

Tulu slid off his horse, then bent over and untied the ropes that held Marie in place on the mule's back. Picking her up, the big man walked away and stepped inside a large, canvas tent.

"Now, this here boy's name is Matthew. He is our new hand. I want you to make him feel welcome and don't give him too much grief, you hear me? You share your grub with him and teach him what he needs to know or I'll hear about it." Randall put his hand on

Mattie's knee, glaring at the faces surrounding them in the twilight.

He turned to his left and said, "And that goes for you too, Top Hat. None of your guff with this youngster, do ya hear?"

Top Hat stared at his cousin's face for a moment, then at Mattie. Saying nothing, he slapped his dusty hat against his thigh and stalked off into the shadows.

The rest of the night passed by in a blur of whispered voices, furtive movements and silent fear. Mattie was led to the fire and a plate of some sort of stew was thrust in his face. An old man who introduced himself as Parker sat down on the ground by his side. He handed the boy an old blanket and asked, "Do you know how to handle horseflesh?"

Mattie nodded silently and Parker said, "You need to speak up, son. I'm hard of hearing. Besides, pouting about your situation will only get you in trouble with this outfit, understand?"

He turned to the man and answered, "Yes, sir. I understand."

"Good." Parker nodded. "You're a young'un, I see, and I'm sorry for whatever happened to bring you to this state. You're in it now, though, and there's no denying it. So you best work hard and give no call to bring more grief your way. I'll see you do things the right way but, if you're too sassy, I'll be telling the boss."

The old man turned to stare at Mattie. In the fire's glow, he saw that Parker's hair was yellowish white and one side of his face looked to be melted like candle wax. His left eye was wide open, though, and stared down at him with concern. Mattie knew he had to trust someone and he thought he saw some kindness in the oldster's remaining eye.

He nodded and replied, "No sir, I won't sass you and I promise to work hard. Thank you."

Parker stared at his charge for a moment and his crusty heart seemed to crack in his chest. This boy bore an uncanny resemblance to his son, dead so many years now he didn't have the numbers at hand to count their passing. He remembered his two girls as well...and his wife, all burned up in the conflagration the Blackfoot Indians made of their home in southern Idaho.

Long-buried memories roared through him, making him feel dizzy with emotions. Then, taking himself firmly in hand, he cleared his throat and stood up. Looking down at the sweet, young boy with green eyes and blond hair that stuck up in tufts on his head, he barked, "You get some shut eye, now. We ride early."

With those words, Parker strode off into the shadows and turned away so the others could not see the steady stream of tears that ran like rain down his withered cheeks.

5

GRACE UNDER PRESSURE

IT FELT LIKE ONLY A FEW MOMENTS HAD PASSED WHEN Mattie opened his eyes to a gray dawn. Tulu crouched over him and hissed, "Better wake up, boy…NOW!"

Sitting bolt upright, Mattie rubbed throbbing eyelids and looked around the camp. He saw that four horses and their riders were already trotting off into the rising sun. However, Randall Penny and a few other men stood by the coals of last night's fire, sipping coffee and smoking.

"Get yerself some of that brew, son, and then come and help me with these horses and those Gawd-dang mules." Parker grinned down at him.

Mattie realized that his new friend was far older than he had thought the night before. His long, white hair fell in one, long braid down his left shoulder. Mattie understood, in the light of day, that most of the man's scalp on the right side was nothing but burnt scar tissue.

"Yes, sir!" Mattie mumbled, and yawned. He had lain awake much of the night, worrying over what had happened, Marie's welfare, and what was to come. He felt like a will o' the wisp, forever caught on life's tumultuous winds, as helpless and ineffectual as a twig floating on rushing waters.

Standing up, Mattie shook his blanket out and folded it twice, placing it neatly on a nearby rock before joining the others by the fire. He studied the smoke-blackened coffeepot for a moment and then spied a piece of leather stropping in the dirt close to the coals. Picking it up, he used it as a potholder and poured himself a swallow or two of the bitter black brew.

"Gawd Almighty!" Daryl exclaimed. "It took Rooster twenty tries and twice the blisters before he figured that trick out!"

"To hell witcha all," muttered a voice from the other side of the fire to a round of snickers.

Randall watched the boy sip his coffee and asked, "Have you been to school, young'un?"

Mattie winced. Somehow, he didn't think that being educated and knowing his arithmetic and letters would ingratiate him to this crew. Still, he didn't think it prudent to lie.

"Yes, sir. My ma taught me to read and write."

"Did she, now?" The man's black and gray eyebrows drew together in a thoughtful frown. "And who are your folks, if I may ask?"

Mattie could practically see the wheels turning in

Penny's head. Education was often costly and usually meant that the families of educated children had money to spare. For once, and despite what his own heart said, Mattie was glad that his ma and pa were gone, along with the family fortune. Never would they be a victim of Randall Penny's greed.

"They are dead now, sir. My pa from a stroke and my ma from the pox." Mattie didn't dare mention his sister but then he, himself, had no idea where Maude was or how to find her. Knowing that his eyes were red and hot with wrath, he hoped his demeanor didn't raise the man's ire. Looking down, he mumbled, "Please sir, I'm supposed to help Mr. Parker. May I be excused?"

"Yes, go to work now," Randall replied, watching as the boy moved swiftly to Parker's side. He had no doubt that Matthew was telling the truth about his folks but he also sensed that the boy was not telling the *whole* truth. *What is it about him that makes me think still waters run deep?*

Tossing the dregs of his coffee onto the dying embers, he thought, *Ah well, if there's a fortune to be had with that boy, I'll ferret it out of him soon enough...and the girl?* He grinned. Annie McCauley would love to have a young new virgin in her stable and would pay well for the privilege.

He looked around and, raising his voice to be heard loud and clear, hollered, "Listen up! I want the wagon and four, plus the mules, to be ready within the hour.

Pack for a six day run into Seattle. And, Parker, pack for cold weather, you hear?"

"Yes sir, I hear ya," Parker answered.

Turning to Mattie, he said, "Son, you go tend to those mules. Feed' em and make damn sure their leathers aren't wet. You will find extra riggin's in that stock wagon over past the tent. Also, grab as many of those buffalo pelts as you can carry and put 'em in back of that wagon over there." The old man pointed south and Mattie saw a newer wagon parked by the cliff's rocky walls.

"Yes, sir!" he said and ran to the older of the two wagons. He saw the leather braces, bits, and harnesses under an oilskin tarp. Throwing a couple sets over one shoulder, he wrestled two heavy skins out of the back and staggered over to the newer wagon. Arms trembling from the effort, he lifted the two skins inside and hurried over to the restive mules.

While he fed, watered and brushed the animals—trying to avoid the bigger one's large, square teeth—he saw Tulu walking slowly behind Marie to the edge of the encampment where a privy had been dug for necessary business.

Studying his friend carefully, Mattie thought she seemed sad but unharmed. Gritting his teeth, he knew why. Although he was still innocent of the congress between men and women, he knew enough to understand that a virgin was a valued commodity...one that Randall Penny would be loath to part with...without being paid for it first anyway.

Then he spied Tulu's broad back, uncovered despite the morning's cool chill. It was completely waffled with whip marks and scar tissue. For all his size, the huge black man had been whipped to his knees over and over again, nigh onto death. Or so it seemed to the boy who stood aghast, his mouth hanging open in shock and pity.

Mattie watched as Tulu directed Marie to the privy, turning around to give the girl some privacy. The big man crossed his arms and stared back at the boy with eyes as dark and fathomless as the deepest sea. He showed no shame or embarrassment but a slow, simmering pride and dignity that made Mattie look quickly away.

His own people came from slave states and took great care of their "folk." His ma had often told him how much she missed her own personal slave named Teeny, and how she had never forgiven her husband for forbidding the woman to accompany her mistress out west.

Mattie had also heard, however, about the cruelty of some white masters and the appalling treatment many Africans had received from slave traders of all nationalities. It appeared Tulu had been the recipient of that terrible treatment and Mattie resolved to be as kind and courteous to the fellow as possible…that is, unless the man tried to make good on his threat of eating him and Marie for dinner. Then he would stab those dark, knowing eyes right out of his head.

Forty-five minutes later, Randall shouted, "That's it,

we're leavin'. Tulu, go fetch that girl. Matthew, you and Parker get in back."

Mattie had no idea where they were headed or why, but he knew better than to delay. He jumped in the back of the wagon alongside Parker and made room for Marie once she arrived. Then—with Penny and his cousin riding on the buckboard and Mattie, Marie and the old man riding shotgun, stuffed in amongst the furs in back—the wagon took off, heading west.

The Sherman Stage Line used to make bi-weekly runs between Wenatchee and Seattle but—due to inclement weather and mechanical breakdowns of its three coaches—that would not be happening this time around. Randall Penny frowned, thinking about the trip ahead of them. He was almost certain he could get a hundred dollars out of the avaricious Madame Annie for the little girl but was it worth traveling through such hostile territory for a measly hundred silvers?

He cursed his luck and his rotten, lousy timing. Who could have known when he and Top Hat left Wyoming for greener pastures in the state of Columbia that the Indians would go to war against one another? The Northwest Trading Company had set the stage with their tainted furs and arrogant proprietorship over what was, so far, still Indian country.

Then the Roman Catholic priests and the Protestant ministers threw dried grass on smoldering coals when they started competing against each other for ownership of the natives' souls. After the massacre at Whitman Mission, Indians turned against one another, blaming first this tribe and then that tribe for the slaughter of the kindly missionaries. Now, the Cayute and Umatilla nations were at war with almost everyone and neither cared who was caught up in their fight.

Oh well, he mused. *There is no crying over spilt milk. This is the life I chose, for good or bad.* Besides, there wasn't just one girl to pawn off for cash; there was a whole shipment of rifles, pistols and whiskey sitting at the Seattle dockyard that he and his cousin could sell for three times the purchase price. He had already sent four of his boys into Spokane Falls to collect protection money owed them from four saloons. That would bring in some much-need money as well.

In addition, Monte, the displaced Nez Perce buck that served as the gang's tracker and arrow man, was headed back into Indian Territory to trade some coffee, whiskey and sugar for native knick-knacks. That kind of stuff always sold well in Spokane and Seattle when trains and wagons of settlers pulled into town. *Sure, the outfit is low on cash right now,* he acknowledged with a sigh, *and the boys are mad because the big payoff at the Dupre' trading post didn't pan out but, as always, we will make do.*

Glancing over at Top Hat, Randall sighed. His cousin was getting worse and worse. Even when he was a youngster, there was something a little off about the way he looked at the world, as if it was his God-given right to beat beast and man into whatever shape he saw fit and goddamn the consequences. Now, though, a keen and perverted cruelty had taken hold of the man.

There was no call for Top Hat to shoot that girl's mother right in front of her eyes. When they had decided to silence the witness to their crime, Randall had no sooner uttered the words than Hat hauled off and did the deed without any thought to the emotional affect it might have on Marie's future value.

He was mean to animals, too, and God help any red Injuns they crossed paths with. Closing his eyes in order to keep his ever-growing revulsion from his face, Randall whispered to himself, "I need to do something about my crazy cousin soon before he brings the whole world and its wrath down upon us all.

6

TOP HAT

Mattie was scooting along a stout branch on top of an apple tree in the backyard. The sky was heavy with yellow-gray clouds and tiny, crystalline drops of hail tapped at the tree's leaves. There were about a dozen more apples to pick and then they could all go back inside where it was warm.

He seized three of the blood-red apples and crowed, "I got a few more…almost done!" Looking down, Mattie saw the open mouths of the burlap sacks his ma and sister held up to catch the falling fruit. He pitched two and snorted in disgust when the bag collapsed.

"Hey! Hold your bag up, Maude, darn it!" Mattie was loath to admit it but his knees went a little shivery when he climbed too high and he was ready for this late autumn harvest to be over and done with.

Yet the bag lay empty on the ground as if Maude had just run off somewhere. Frustrated, Mattie looked around and saw the bottom of his ma's skirt. Frowning, he noticed how dirty her apron was. *What in blazes has she been doing?* He wondered.

He saw her hold up her sack but, although he leaned this way and that, he couldn't see her face.

"Mattie!" she cried. "Mattie, can you help me?"

"Sure, Ma! Just give me a second to climb outta this tree," he said. Tossing the last apple, he started down. But when he reached the ground, both sacks were there, still empty.

"Ma...Maudie, where are you?" Mattie hollered. It was snowing heavily now and he pulled his jacket closed with chilled fingers.

"Mattie!" His ma was calling him again but this time her voice was far away. "Mattie, help us, please..."

His heart was breaking in fear and tears were freezing to his cheeks. He wanted to help but knew, somehow, that he couldn't. He covered his ears when her call came one last time...then he opened his eyes with a gasp.

Marie was leaning over him with a small green apple in one hand. Tiny, dry aspen leaves were raining down on them with a soft patter.

"I've been calling you and calling you, Mattie, but you were sleeping hard," Marie said. "Here are some apples Tulu picked for us. Are you hungry?"

He smiled at the fruit held under his nose and glanced over the rails of the wagon at Tulu riding his big roan close by. He was talking softly to Parker who sat high on one of the rolled up buffalo pelts, a rifle cradled casually across his chest.

Wiping an errant tear, he croaked and cleared his throat. "Hi. I'm glad you're awake. Are you feeling better?"

Marie took a small nibble of an apple and sighed.

"Oui...I guess so." Her shoulders drooped and she shrugged, looking away.

Mattie took her hand, seeing that dried blood still stained her cuffs and the bottom of her brown gingham dress. He whispered, "Have they hurt you?"

She shook her head, and her long, black curls shone blue in the sunlight. "No...except for, well, you know."

"Enough talk outta you two!" Top Hat snarled.

Mattie saw that Randall was asleep; his mouth hung open on his chest and his head bobbed back and forth in rhythm with the horse's steps. Top Hat was turned around in his seat, glaring at them with cold, snake-like eyes.

Suddenly, Tulu spurred his horse. He trotted to the front of the wagon and mumbled, "Sumpin' you need, Boss?"

"Nah. You just make sure those two pups don't get up to something while my back's turned, you hear?"

Top Hat looked at them and scowled again. "You!" he barked, pointing at Marie. "You get up here behind us...and keep your mouth shut."

Marie blushed and scrambled over the hides to the front of the wagon directly behind Randall. She settled in so that the only thing Mattie could see of her was her eyes. Turning to Parker, Mattie asked, "Where are we, do you know?"

"We're about fifty miles northeast of Wenatchee, son." He took an old rag from his back pocket and wetted it with water from his canteen. Handing the damp cloth to the boy, he added, "I want you ter wash up and keep a sharp eye out, alright?"

Mattie nodded and started running the washrag over his face, neck and ears. Gazing around at the landscape, he saw sagebrush and arid plains. He also saw tall pine and fir trees in the distance and realized they appeared to be headed toward a mountain range that rose like a giant serrated saw in the far distance. He had always admired the smaller peaks of home known as the Bitterroots and the Saddleback Mountains but they were tiny hillocks compared to what loomed in front of them now.

His heart started beating hard in his chest and he asked the old man, "Sir, is that Seattle?"

"So, you heard the boss say we are going to Seattle, did ya?"

When Mattie nodded, Parker shrugged. "Well, you heard right. We're going into that city for supplies and...other things. But that there is the Cascade mountain range. There is a road cut through it but you need to understand that it's rough country. There are bears and mountain lions and all manner of critters up in those hills that would like to eat us for supper."

Looking sideways at his young charge, Parker asked, "Can you handle a rifle, boy?"

Mattie replied, "Yes, sir. My pa taught me."

Suddenly, Top Hat pulled back on the reins and

yelled, "Whoa...whoa, you nags!" The wagon came to a stop and he glared in displeasure.

"That kid will not be holdin' no firearms, Parker. Have you gone loco on us in your old age?"

"My cousin here, he has a soft heart," he continued through clenched teeth. "But me? I know better than to trust these whelps...and so should you!" Gesturing down at Marie, Top Hat added, "This one would put a knife to my throat, given half a chance!"

Mattie, watching the exchange with alarm, saw something dark pass over the man's face, like storm clouds racing past the sun. He pressed his body against Parker's back.

Top Hat studied Parker's face, then leaned over with a bitter grimace and spat on the ground. "Or just maybe that's what you want, eh? I know you never did like me overmuch, you old coot but, if I think you're cooking up something behind my back, I'll..."

"Shut the fuck up, Top Hat!"

Randall had come fully awake and sat staring at his cousin with a red face. Reaching over, he grabbed the traces out of Top Hat's hands.

"I think it's about time you got some shut eye! We are all tired but no one is plottin' nuthin' and I won't have you threatening my best hand, hear me?"

Top Hat stared at Parker a moment longer before he turned around and leaned back against the wagon rails.

Mattie did not miss the raw fear in Parker's eyes, the sudden tension in Tulu's shoulders, or Randall

Penny's panicked reaction to a situation that very nearly got out of hand over nothing while he was asleep.

Vowing to watch out for Top Hat just as much as the wild animals Parker warned of, Mattie settled down in the middle of the wagon bed as they headed west.

A couple of hours later, Randall pulled the horses to a stop and said, "Everybody out! We'll take some lunch here and fill our canteens with water."

Mattie had needed to pee for a couple of hours but didn't have the nerve to say anything. As soon as the wagon's wheels came to a stop, he sprang out the back. Intending to empty his bladder behind one of the closest trees, he was brought up short with a yell.

"Hey! Don't be runnin' off! You stay close!" It was Top Hat again, who had rattled the wagon's boards for the last two hours with his snores.

Randall rolled his eyes and said, "Leave him alone, cousin. Don't you see he's about to piss himself?"

"Jes' sayin, Boss…" Top Hat muttered, gazing at Mattie with hot eyes.

Mattie hurried behind a smallish pine and sighed with relief as he wet the ground in front of his boots. Looking through the tree's needles, he watched as Tulu led Marie behind a large boulder; he saw Parker rummaging around in a leather sack for some grub and Randall rubbing the aches out of his lower back…he didn't see Top Hat anywhere. Suddenly nervous,

Mattie buttoned his britches and started back toward the wagon but a tall form stepped in his path.

Top Hat stood there with a strange look on his face. There was hunger there—and greed—but there was something else, too. Something Mattie didn't understand. The man had his pants opened and clutched his personals in one hand while he burned holes in Mattie's body with his eyes.

Top Hat's cheeks were flushed and his eyes wide with excitement. He leered and whispered, "Where you headed, boy? Come over here."

Mattie had once done the thing Top Hat was doing when he daydreamed about Marie and he almost died from the shame of it. His cheeks turned red now as he realized what was happening and that the boss's cousin was a sodomite with designs upon him.

Stepping sideways, Mattie jinked through a small stand of jack pines and ran back toward the wagon. He saw Tulu watch his approach and stare past him toward the sheltering trees.

"You stay by me and old man Parker, you hear me?" Tulu murmured.

Mattie nodded his head, willing his hands to stop shaking as he gathered up their canteens.

7

TRIAL BY FIRE

THEY TRAVELED ANOTHER SIX HOURS UNTIL, FINALLY, Mattie saw a small town in the distance just as the sun was fixing to go to bed. His heart leapt in nervous excitement. He could imagine grabbing Marie and running into one of the houses on the outskirts. Shacks and tents mainly but, still, the warm lantern light shining through the cracks of those structures seemed like beacons of safety and comfort.

Unfortunately, Top Hat pulled up short of the perimeter and the horses stamped their hooves in agitation. There was a large stockyard at the far edge of the town limits where Mattie could hear cows lowing as hay and grain were spread out for the livestock.

Randall and his cousin climbed down from the wagon and conferred together quietly. Mattie stared at the houses again and tried to think of a way to escape his captors until Tulu rode up to the side of the wagon. The big man stared into Mattie's face and shook his head slightly as though he could read the thoughts racing through the boy's mind as easily as words on paper.

Mattie sighed and scooted back down into the bison hides. Staring over at where Marie sat gazing back at him, he shrugged his shoulders in defeat and saw that she understood his thwarted intentions and frustration. Then Randall walked up to where Tulu and Parker stood by the back of the wagon.

"Unhitch the horses, Parker, and get two saddled up. Top Hat and I are headed into that town to pick up supplies and extra grain for the animals." Staring at Mattie, he added, "You be good, Matthew, and don't you be thinkin' about runnin' off."

"Yes, sir," Mattie answered.

Turning around, Randall said, "Tulu, I would rather you came with us but I don't know if ol' Parker is quick enough to stop these pups if they jack-rabbit. Besides, I need you here to guard against any Injuns. There are plenty around here and they're all riled up from fightin' each other. I don't think they'd be bothered by scalpin' themselves a nigger and a couple of white kids if they took a mind to stealin' this wagon and the animal flesh we've got."

"Yes, suh. I'll keep an eye out," Tulu mumbled.

Mattie gazed out into the darkness surrounding them and shivered. Randall and his pervert cousin were bad enough. Now every shrub, tree and boulder took on the look of fighting braves with tomahawks, spears and feathered bows and arrows...every one of them intent on the murder of two lost children.

"Alright. We'll be back in a few hours and, Parker, no fire tonight!"

With those words, the two outlaws rode off toward town. After the sound of the horse's hooves faded into the distance, Parker said, "Okay, you two. Get down from that wagon. You can do your necessaries and stretch your legs a bit. Then I got some cold beans for dinner." He paused. "But like the boss said, don't go runnin' off. Randall wasn't lying, ya know. The Indians around these parts would love nothin' better than to take you kids for trade. Once they got you, you're gone fer good."

"I'll watch 'em, Parker," Tulu said, stepping down off his horse.

Mattie couldn't help but be glad. A coyote started yipping and its pack mates took up the cry. It sounded as if the animals were just a few feet away from the wagon and he couldn't help but wonder if those critters might be so bold as to gang up and attack one of them for dinner.

"Those dogs are a long ways off," Tulu said as if Mattie had spoken out loud. Though, looking up at the tall man, the boy thought his guard sounded scared, too.

All three of them took care of business and then walked back to the wagon where Parker had set three plates on the backboard. Cold beans, biscuits and jerky...the same meal as the last three they had eaten.

Mattie and Marie sat on the ground close to Parker; Tulu walked into the shadows and stood close to his horse. Mattie saw that he was feeding bits of biscuit to his mount while staring suspiciously out at the shadowy landscape.

Parker lit a lantern and turned the wick down low. Pulling a blanket up over his shoulders, he brought the lantern close to his crossed legs so what little light there was cast eerie shadows on the old man's face and fuzzy white braid. Looking up, he studied the children and asked, "How you kids holdin' up?"

Marie just blinked in silence but Mattie, who sensed that the old man was an ally, said, "We're okay, sir."

Parker bent over his tin plate and scooped the beans in his mouth with dogged determination as if this might be his last meal. For all Mattie knew, with what was happening, it might well be.

The old man scooped up the rest of his meal, then whispered, "You two just be good and hold on tight, ya hear?" Glancing back at Tulu, he added, "I happen to know that the boss is about ready to retire. He just needs one more big pay day to do it, see?"

He stared at Marie for a moment, the burnt scar tissue on his face writhing like snakes in the lantern's fitful glow.

"I, fer one, am sorry 'bout what happened to yer folks, girl. Top Hat…" Parker curled his lips and spat. "He had no call to shoot yer ma in front of you the way he done."

Marie's eyes filled with tears as bright as sapphires and Mattie took her hand in his. Glaring up at Parker, he said, "Randall Penny is nothing but a thief and a murderer!"

Parker gazed at Mattie thoughtfully and nodded. "I guess you're right about that, son. But he wasn't always like that. Sometimes life takes a strange road and turns a man into something...bad. Just remember this, though, before you get up on yer high horse. Dupre shot first. If'n he woulda just handed over what he had without gun play, then he might still be alive today and this girl would be safe at home in her mother's arms."

"He didn't have anything! The payroll hadn't come in yet!" Mattie insisted.

"Well, maybe you shoulda spoke up then and told the boss what you knew!"

Parker was angry now and Mattie didn't want to lose the one friend he had amongst this band of thieves. He looked down and whispered, "I'm sorry, sir, you're right. I should have said something."

Parker gazed into the lantern light for a moment and sighed. "No, you're right. Nothin' you said woulda changed what happened, son. In fact, Top Hat prob'ly would have shot you for sheer meanness. It's Top Hat what changed Randall Penny from a legitimate businessman into what he is now."

Tulu suddenly appeared out of the shadows. "Horses coming this way, Parker...and fast!"

Looking alarmed, Parker said, "You kids scramble now. Hurry!"

Taking Marie's hand, Mattie jumped into the wagon, pulling her in with him. Then he stared out into the dark and heard the sound of horses approaching at a full gallop. Parker and Tulu stood in rigid attention with rifles at the ready.

Mattie was shaking with fear; he couldn't stand being unable to see who was coming. It could be Randall and Top Hat or another group of outlaws, or even Indians!

"That's Top Hat, Parker, but it looks like he's leading the boss's horse. Get ready to move, quick!" Tulu mounted his horse and trotted toward the approaching riders.

Mattie strained his eyes and, sure enough, he saw Top Hat's showy Appaloosa gelding come to a skidding stop in front of them. Penny's mare was blowing and crow-hopping as Tulu attempted to catch her reins with one hand and help Randall out of his saddle with the other.

Randall groaned as he slid into Tulu's arms. The big man lowered his boss to the ground and Mattie saw that the front of his shirt was wet and shiny with what could only be blood. Parker, who had led the panicked horse away, rushed back with the lantern and gasped when he saw Penny's injury.

"Knife wound...what the hell happened?" Parker demanded.

Top Hat was busily tying the mare to the back of the wagon with a long lead rope. She was covered in blood and shuddered, tossing her head with nerves but he was having none of it. Hauling back a fist, he punched the animal hard on the muzzle. She subsided at once, hanging her head in defeat.

Top Hat turned to Parker and growled, "It's a long story and I don't have time to tell it. We got to get outta here so you need to get Randall in back of this wagon. We're leaving now!"

Tulu lifted Penny up in his arms while Mattie cleared some of the buffalo hides to one side to make room for the old man's body. No sooner had Tulu and Mattie placed Randall in the wagon, Parker yelled, "Hah!"

The horses lunged against the traces and Mattie saw Tulu run back to mount his gelding. As the wagon and two riders rode swiftly uphill toward the lower slopes of the Cascade Mountains, the boy and girl used rags to staunch the blood seeping slowly but steadily out of the old outlaw's chest.

It was just past midnight on Mattie's thirteenth birthday.

Redbird rode his pony slowly, following the hoof prints and blood trail of the men who had tortured and killed his brother the night before.

He and his little brother, Moses Sky Dreamer, were chosen to go to the white man's settlement this month for supplies. Redbird hated going to town and resented the looks of scorn and hatred that greeted their every move. They were treated as if they were beneath contempt although, in his mind, it was the whites in their dirty, stinking aprons and foul breath who were shameful.

Still, every brave in his small village was tasked with the chore and Redbird would not have it whispered that he shirked his duties.

Things had gone well enough until it was time to go into one of the three saloons to buy a half case of whiskey for the tribal elders and their medicine man. The brothers picked the drinking establishment closest to the stockyard, both for the fact that their ponies were close by and the owner of the bar seemed like a kindly man who showed some respect for the Nez Perce traders on their monthly excursions.

Redbird always allowed himself one small glass of the firewater before he left to go back home and last night was no exception. He had sent Moses Sky Dreamer out to fetch the ponies and stood sipping the amber liquid, relishing the burnt taste and wishing he had not promised his sibling a taste.

He waited, frowning angrily. That boy was indeed a dreamer! He should have been back by now but was probably staring up at the sky, as usual, and lost track of time. As punishment, Redbird finished his drink in one gulp, picked up the box of whiskey and walked out the open, canvas door of the big tent.

Looking up and down the dirt lane, the Indian saw no sign of his brother or their ponies. Sighing with disgust, he shouldered the wooden crate of bottles and trudged up the street toward the stables.

Then he heard a sound, a muffled cry of pain.

Fearing the worst, he set the box on the ground. Creeping toward the wide, wooden rails of the stable gates, he saw something almost unbelievable.

A tall, skinny white man had his little brother bent over at the waist, a long bowie knife pressed against his neck. This was bad enough but what made him shiver in disgust and rage was that the man was obviously taking his brother from behind like a dog with its bitch. Unbidden, Redbird screamed a war cry and ran towards them.

Just then, another white man—having apparently heard the Indian war whoop—rushed around the back of one of the stalls and cried, "What in tarna..." Randall's eyes took in what his cousin was doing.

"My God, Kevin! I knew you was getting worse but this...this is..." Penny was at a loss for words. "Let the boy go, cousin," Randall finished, eyeing the older Indian who stood framed in the lantern light close by the front door.

Kevin Walker—better known as Top Hat for the greasy old hat he always wore—grinned and said, "If'n that Injun makes one move, I'll slit this one's throat from stem to root!"

Randall lifted his rifle, pointing it at his cousin. "Are you outta your mind? Do you really think that these two are on their own? Look at those ponies, Kevin!" Randall was white-eyed with fear. "They're on a supply run, don't you see? Their tribe is prob'ly only miles away!"

Redbird understood only one word in ten of the

older man's speech but he brandished his knife, hoping against hope that the skinny one would let his little brother go.

But Top Hat just smiled and ran his knife across Moses' throat. The youngster's eyes grew wide and he collapsed to the ground in a puddle of blood. Letting out a war cry of his own, Kevin sprang backwards even as Randall rushed in to help the young brave.

In that same instant, Redbird let his throwing knife loose and it sank hilt deep into the older man's chest. Looking around, the Indian saw that the skinny man with big, bucked teeth like a beaver's was hidden out of sight.

He stared down at his brother—who stared sightlessly back—and at the older man who was trying to staunch the blood that ran out of his chest in sheets. Knowing he had to get away before the white men in town hanged him for his crimes and fearing for his tribe's safety, Redbird cut the supplies from his pony and galloped out of town.

Now—as the Indian walked around a trampled area noting wheel tracks, hoof prints and footprints— Redbird swore vengeance upon the men who had murdered his brother.

8

COLD TO THE BONE

MANY HOURS LATER AS THE SKY TURNED A MURKY GRAY, Mattie pressed another rag to Randall's chest and he rolled his eyes, panting against the agony. Shortly after the group made its mad dash up into the foothills, rain had begun to fall. Softly at first, it now poured in soaking torrents, causing the rolled up buffalo hides to cast a stench in the air that mingled with the urine and feces in Penny's pants as he wrestled with death.

"What Maman said was true," Marie whispered fearfully as she held her skirt over Randall's head to keep the rain out of his eyes. "She said she saw L'Ange de Mort sitting on this man's shoulder." Mattie looked up into his friend's eyes and saw her shiver with superstitious dread.

He nodded, not knowing what to say except, "Do you have a dry cloth left? This rag is soaked."

Marie bent over and ripped another piece of her skirt away. It was none too clean but it wasn't like there were many options at this point. Randall seemed calmer suddenly and he gazed up at Mattie with a tranquil expression.

Alarmed, Mattie hollered, "Mr. Parker, sir! We need to stop! It's Mr. Penny...I think he's getting worse!"

Tulu reined his horse in and Mattie heard Parker shout, "Whoa, whoa..." The wagon came to a stop. Parker turned around on the driver's seat as Tulu got off his horse and prepared to jump in back. Just then, Penny's hand came up and grabbed Mattie's arm.

"Boy! You gotta listen up," he gasped.

Mattie took the man's hand and whispered, "I am listening, sir."

Penny nodded and swallowed. "Top Hat...my cousin, Kevin, he..." Suddenly, the man's body trembled violently and went rigid. He bucked and shivered, his eyes rolling in his head like a loco horse. Even as Mattie and Tulu tried to still the man's tremors, the boy saw Penny's face turn as white as a sheet in the early morning light.

He quieted then and his eyes were lucid as he stared up into the falling rain. "Top Hat raped and killed an Indian boy. The tribe..." He coughed and blood spilled over his lips. "They'll be coming after us fer sure..."

Then he was gone. Mattie stared down at the man's face as his spirit fled while Tulu met Parker's eyes in grave understanding. Marie crawled back to her place behind Parker and covered her head with one of the buffalo pelts. Then they all heard hoof beats as Top Hat trotted back to the wagon.

"What the hell is going on here, Parker?" Top Hat stared at the old man who gazed back at him with a sullen expression in his one wrinkled eye then walked his horse around to the side of the wagon and peered in at his dead cousin. "Well, hell," he muttered, spitting on the ground in disgust.

Mattie stared at Top Hat in shock. There did not seem to be one ounce of remorse in the man's eyes or grief over Randall's passing.

Tulu, on the other hand, wept openly and mumbled, "The boss...he save me. Gave me a job and money so I be a free man." Lowering his big head, he sobbed into his hands.

Top Hat sneered, rolling his eyes. Turning to Parker, he said, "We gotta keep going. It's a shame what happened but, if'n we don't find shelter and soon, we'll all be dead jes' like my cousin here."

Parker glared and his face turned an alarming shade of red. "And why is that, Top Hat?" he asked. "How is it that a simple trip to town turned so hazardous, huh?"

Mattie stared back and forth between the two men, biting his lip in fear. It was a valid question but Mattie knew that Parker was playing with fire. Top Hat had been riding point when Randall spilled the beans so he couldn't know that the rest of the party was aware of his actions. But if Parker didn't let up soon, he would tip his hand and Mattie had no doubt Top Hat would silence every single one of them if that happened.

Daring to speak out loud, Mattie said, "I'm with Mr. Top Hat, sir. We should get going!"

Parker studied Mattie's face for a second, then faced front again with a grimace of rage. Slapping the reins on the horse's rumps, he cried, "Giddap!"

The wagon jerked forward. Mattie saw Tulu standing in the rain by his horse, as if undecided whether or not to accompany them. But just as the scanty road veered left around a corner, Mattie saw the big man jump on his horse and follow.

He pulled one of the hides across Penny's body and over his dead, staring eyes. Shivering, he wondered what would happen next since it seemed as though the evil Top Hat was now in charge.

They pulled into a clearing about five hours later. The rain had stopped for the moment and a chill breeze whipped the forest's treetops and whistled a strange, mournful tune as if ghosts were dancing and singing in the needled branches.

Marie had woken up and scooted to the side of the wagon, looking out at an old, abandoned cabin. Nestled in the pine trees it looked like a dirty, lonesome sort of place but they needed to rest the animals. In addition, Mattie spied the stones of an old chimney. Perhaps they could all get warm and dry before night fell.

He felt cold droplets kiss his cheeks. Looking up, Mattie saw that the rain had turned to snow. A dark pall was rising in the sky to the west and he realized that this ramshackle cabin might keep them all from freezing to death out in the open.

"Matthew, grab a few of those skins and haul 'em

inside." Parker had climbed off the wagon seat and was unbuckling the horses from their traces. "Girl, you head on in and try to get a fire started. I see some branches and pinecones by the front door…hurry!"

Marie nodded and ran toward the cabin. Top Hat sat his horse looking back at the winding trail from whence they came; he took off his hat and slapped it against his thigh. Turning around, he walked his horse toward the wagon and then pulled up short, staring back down the trail.

He hollered over the wind, "Tulu, I'm gonna shoot us a couple of rabbits for dinner. You watch out fer those young'uns. I'll be back soon."

Mattie hauled four hides into the cabin and then scrimmaged around the bottom of the woodpile for dry twigs and pinecones for the fire. Snow was falling steadily now, small dry pellets of ice that painted the ground white. The temperature was falling as well and Mattie shivered in relief. This wayside cabin was a godsend.

Parker stepped up on the porch with his arms full of tack and leather bundles of supplies. Mattie saw that Tulu had sheltered the mules and horses close to the cabin away from the wind and driving snow. Two rain barrels sat under the eaves and the animals dipped their noses in deep for long draughts of water.

""Come on, kid, afore yer freeze yer ass off!" Parker shouted.

Mattie stepped in the door, Tulu close behind. They spent some time getting situated; helping Marie with the fire, giving Parker a hand with the coffee pot and victuals, spreading the hides across the floor close by the stove.

Finally, after shedding their wet clothes and sipping strong, black coffee to get warm, Parker spoke. "Reckon he skedaddled?"

Tulu nodded, staring into the flames of the potbelly stove. "Reckon so."

Parker heaved a sigh. "Yellow-belly fucker...excuse my language, Sis," he grumbled.

Mattie had almost forgotten about Top Hat in the rush of finding shelter from the storm. Now that he remembered, though, he was glad. He trusted Parker. He even felt safe around the huge, silent Negro. Top Hat was the threat and always had been so Mattie rejoiced that he was gone.

The fire warmed the air; the buff hides thawed and discarded clothing steamed in one corner of the room. Marie yawned, curling up with her back to the stove. Within minutes, Parker was snoring as well. Mattie looked at Tulu who sat gazing at a leather-covered window opening. There was such sorrow on the man's features Mattie could not bear to look.

"Will you help me bury Mr. Penny tomorrow, Matthew?" Tulu whispered into the silence.

"Yes, sir," Mattie answered. He had no doubt that Tulu could carve a grave out of the ground with his own bare hands, but the big man seemed almost frightened of the prospect of burying his friend alone without someone there to stand witness.

Silence crept over the cabin, and snow fell long into the night as Mattie and the others slept.

"Wake up, son!"

Mattie blinked in the gloom and saw shadowed figures moving swiftly in the woodstove's firelight glow.

Sitting up, he asked, "What's going on? Is Top Hat back?"

"Shhh!" It was Parker, leaning over him with a shotgun in his hand. He held the gun out to Mattie and the boy saw that the old man's one good eye was wide with fear.

"Tulu thinks it's an Indian raiding party, son. Now you know and I know that we didn't do nuthin wrong but those bucks out there won't care whether we be innocent or not." Parker curled his lips and spat at the fire. "Goddamn that cur, Top Hat!" he swore. "Took off and left us to pay for his crime!"

Parker moved away and Mattie got to his feet with the shotgun in his hand. Marie was feeding what little firewood they had left to the stove so the room blazed bright with heat. There was a wooden bar across the front door but the door itself was as thin as paper. Mattie dragged a table in front of it, hoping that it might buy them some time if needed.

Staring out at the early morning through a chink in the log wall, he saw at least twenty ponies and their riders riding in circles in front of the cabin. The horse's hooves kicked up clouds of snow and Mattie gaped in awe, not only at the Indians and their pinto ponies but also at the two feet of snow that had fallen while he slept.

One particularly fierce-looking customer was painted red all over as though he had been dipped in blood. He alone stood still, facing the cabin. Raising one hand, he called out something in his own tongue. His comrades slowed their mounts and waited by his side.

"You know what he said, Parker?" Tulu hissed from one corner by the far side of the window.

"Yeah, I think so." Parker sighed. "He said, 'Come out rapist'...or close to that, anyway."

Mattie saw one young brave slide off his horse and run quickly up to the side of the cabin where their animals were hobbled. A few moments later, they were loose and milling around with the Indian ponies where they were quickly caught and tied together in a bunch.

"What do we do, Parker?" For all his size, Tulu deferred leadership to Parker, who shook his head.

"We surrender. That's what we do, Tulu," the old man said softly.

Mattie glanced up when he heard something creak across the mud and dried-grass roof overhead. There was a clatter and Mattie peered out front again as two of the braves yelled in derisive laughter. There was a hollow rumble and then smoke started pouring back down out of the stovepipe and into the cabin. Instantly, Mattie's eyes began to water and his throat slammed shut.

Marie squealed with fear and all four of them

started whooping and coughing, Smoke was so thick, Mattie couldn't see an inch in front of his face. A big hand seized his arm and then there was the scrape of wood on wood as someone dragged the table away from the doorway.

Light filtered in through the escaping smoke. Although Mattie's eyes still stung with tears, he saw the Indians lined up in a row facing the cabin and almost every one of them held their bows and arrows at the ready.

Parker stuck a pair of long johns on a stick out the front door and, coughing, he hollered, "We surrender! Hey! You hear me? We surrender. Don't shoot!"

Turning around, he gazed through the hazy air and said, "You guys stay in here as long as you can. Now that the door is open, they'll come in and fetch you easy instead of burning you out." He looked at Mattie and his good eye winked. "I'm gonna go soften 'em up fer ya…"

"Parker!" Tulu exclaimed but the old man had stepped outside.

Mattie's vision was clear enough now to watch as at least a dozen arrows entered his friend's body before Parker fell backwards with a crash into the cabin.

9

SLINGSHOT

THREE THINGS HAPPENED SIMULTANEOUSLY.

Tulu, who had his rifle pointed up and over Parker's shoulder, stumbled when the old man slammed into him. His rifle roared but his aim was off and the large caliber bullet blew a hole in one of the ceiling braces. Grass, wood splinters and snow filled the air, raining down on them. The interior of the cabin brightened as three braves suddenly flew through the window opening. Mattie heard Marie scream and he lifted his shotgun only to have it plucked out of his hands by one of the Indians.

In the ensuing silence, Mattie heard a whisper. Looking down at Parker, he saw the old man gasping for breath. But his gaze was fixed on Mattie's face and one arm reached his way. "Tom...Tommy, is that you?"

"It's Mattie, sir," he whispered. Yet he knew that Parker had spoken his last words, that whatever spirit had caused him to see another boy in his final moments had fled.

Abruptly, Mattie was lifted into the air from behind and carried outside. He struggled and squirmed but the hands that held him tossed him on the dirt directly in front of the "red" Indian's pony. The painted horse rose up in alarm and kicked out his two front hooves, one of them dealing Mattie's head a glancing blow; he shrieked and tried to scramble out of harm's way.

Mattie briefly lost consciousness but a sharp, nauseating pain woke him and he started retching into the snow. As he puked, Mattie saw blood splatter around him and knew the pony had dealt him a grievous blow. He closed his eyes for a second to stop the dizzy whirling but they opened again when he heard Marie scream. Blubbering in terror, she sobbed, "Mattie! Oh, Mon Dieu...no!"

Struggling to sit up, Mattie watched as an Indian trussed her up on a horse. He tried to rise and run to her but a moccasin-clad foot pushed him back down into the snow. Then he heard a howl of agony. Turning his pounding head carefully to the left, he saw several Indians wrestling Tulu to his knees. The big man was putting up a hell of a fight but there were simply too many. As Mattie watched, the large Negro fell to his knees.

Laughter and harsh war cries filled the air. The red-painted Indian grinned and got down off his horse. Strolling over to where Tulu knelt in the snow, the

Indian picked up one of the black man's long, fuzzy braids and said something to his triumphant braves.

A young man shouted for joy and pulled a long knife out of his cloth belt. Mattie recognized him as the one who had set their livestock free and, later, threw rocks down the chimney pipe. It looked like he was being rewarded for his efforts now and Mattie swallowed against his grief and fear as the boy started sawing at Tulu's scalp.

Tulu wailed, staring at Mattie in horror. Suddenly, he remembered the slingshot in his back pocket. He had been trying for the last four days to find a good time and place to use it but there were always too many guns and too many eyes watching his every move. He had honestly expected the slingshot to be seized but had begun to think that it was overlooked or forgotten.

On the other hand, he thought now, maybe Tulu and Parker did me a kindness and wanted me to have some sort of protection since I wasn't allowed a gun. Well, it is my turn to repay Tulu with a kindness of my own...

The Indian boy was making a mess of things with Tulu's scalp and the big man was squealing with anguish. Blood ran down the man's face and his eyes were full of tears. Mattie reached into his back pocket with one hand, grabbing hold of his slingshot and two, perfectly round stones.

He looked around, nodding in satisfaction. No one was paying him any mind. Marie was turned away from the horrifying scene and Mattie could see her shoulders heaving with sobs. The other braves whooped and hollered, jumping up and down with excitement and laughing.

Mattie ignored the pounding in his head and the blood that obscured the vision in his left eye, trickling into his mouth. Lifting the slingshot, he sighted in on Tulu's temple. His focus became narrow as he calculated the distance and the trajectory. If he was going to ruin the Indian's fun and probably die for his efforts, he needed to get it right.

For a second, Tulu's cries eased off as he caught sight of Mattie and what the boy was trying to do; he nodded once and commenced to screaming again. Mattie took a deep, steadying breath and let his stone fly. Tulu's cries were silenced instantly and the Negro fell over dead in the snow. A hush fell over the clearing and the Indian boy stared at Mattie in shock and anger. Then he snarled, grabbed his tomahawk and ran at Mattie with murder in his eyes.

Mattie closed his eyes against his own death and waited for the ax to fall but he heard a sharp command. Many of the Indian braves had moved in his direction but now they all stood stock-still as the large, red-painted Indian came and stood over Mattie's cowering body.

Reaching down, Redbird snatched the slingshot out of Mattie's grasp and turned it over in his hands. Smiling slightly, he put it in his belt pouch. He gestured at Mattie and then spoke in his native tongue to his fellow fighters. Mattie had no idea what the man was saying but the braves mumbled in wide-eyed respect and backed away.

Gazing down at the boy, Redbird frowned and said, "You got big medicine?" The Indian spoke slowly, laboriously, as though struggling with the white man's unruly words but Mattie understood and nodded.

Redbird studied Mattie's face. He had meant to take all these men's scalps in revenge for his brother and thought the boy's bright, blond hair was particularly attractive but now he wondered. He had seen the teenager sit up, take aim and shoot his stone at the big, black man to devastating effect even as his own blood ran down his face and blinded his vision.

Something strange danced in the boy's eyes at that moment, something mystical and wise that Redbird wanted no part of. He stepped back and looked around. One old man lay still in the cabin's doorway and the white girl with clouds of long, black hair was secured tightly on his cousin's horse. *She will make a good trade,* he thought.

The black man lay dead in the snow and still another body lay frozen and stiff in back of the wagon. It was the man he, himself, had killed after his little brother's throat was cut open. The golden-haired boy stared up at him from the ground with haunted eyes.

Glaring, Redbird bent over and asked, "Where's the other man?" Not having the words he needed, the Indian used his hands to sketch the outline of a tall hat on his own head.

Mattie wondered for a moment what the brave was doing and then his eyes got big, "You mean Top Hat?"

The Indian nodded and answered, "Yes, the hat man."

Mattie shrugged and said, "He's gone...he left yesterday."

Redbird did not understand 'yesterday' but he knew the word 'gone' and believed the boy's words. The Indian gauged his revenge by gazing around at the dead one last time and then shouted something to the others. They moved swiftly toward their ponies and mounted up.

The war party spun their horses around and around where Mattie sat in the bloody snow. They shouted their victory, keeping a safe distance from the dangerous boy and brandished their weapons in the air. Then—with one final flourish—Redbird reared up his pony, hollered something, and rode away.

The last thing Mattie heard was Marie's anguished cry calling out to him before he fell down in a dead faint.

Mattie woke up later with snow falling in his eyes and clogging his nose. Dried blood had hardened into a thick mask on his face and he sat up with a groggy gasp.

"Ow!" he groaned, putting his hand up to the cut on his head. He felt around and found a flap of skin peeled away from his scalp. He knew even as he touched it that fresh blood was starting to flow from the wound again.

He gazed at the devastation and unbidden tears fell from his eyes. Three dead bodies kept him company: Randall Penny, still in the back of the wagon covered in mounds of snow; old man Parker; and Tulu. Mattie allowed himself a small bit of pride. Although his stone had killed the man, he knew that Tulu would have died anyway. His shot had flown true, putting the big man out of his misery.

Sighing, Mattie struggled to his feet and tried to keep from vomiting again. He staggered in place for a moment and then made his way over to where Tulu lay dead in his own frozen blood. He gazed about, wondering what to do, and then he remembered the kerosene in a small metal receptacle in the cabin.

Walking slowly, he made his way up onto the porch and stepped over Parker's body. He saw the small tin jug close to the woodstove and—groaning—bent over to pick it up. Sticking it in his back pocket, Mattie found his jacket and put it on before leaning over and grabbing hold of the old man's ankles.

Grunting with painful exertion, the boy strained backwards and began dragging Parker's body out the door onto the porch. Blood was flowing freely down his face again and Mattie wiped it away with a snarl of annoyance.

Stepping quickly down the one wooden step, he cringed when the old man's grizzled head bounced hard on the wooden slat...then the snow acted as a sled. Mattie dragged Parker close to the wagon and stood still for a moment as his chest hitched and more of his own blood painted the snow pink.

Mattie groaned as he looked over at Tulu's corpse. He just didn't know if he had enough strength to drag that huge body the twenty feet or so to the wagon but he knew he had to try. He walked away and stood still for a second, staring down at the Negro's wide brown eyes.

For some reason, Tulu's scalp had been thrown aside like a piece of rubbish; Mattie bent and picked it up. There was only a small patch of flesh on this particular skein of hair but, for some reason, Mattie did not have the heart to throw it away. Brushing the snow off the long curly lock, Mattie wrapped it around his hand like a piece of rope and put it in his pocket.

Then be knelt in the snow, picked up the man's ankles and let out a cry of pain and sorrow as he pulled with all his might. It took a long time but Mattie finally placed Tulu's body close to Parker's.

Although he was trembling from head to toe, Mattie understood that he needed to finish the job before he gave up altogether. He clutched the wooden slats behind the wagon and crawled inside. His chest heaved with effort and his eyes danced with stars but he managed to scoop most of the snow off Randall Penny's body.

He poked around, trying to see if there was anything useful and found a good rope and an empty canteen. Whispering an apology, Mattie also searched Penny's pockets for money but only found a couple of coins. Sitting back on his heels, he remembered how Top Hat had rummaged around his cousin's body on the pretense of paying his respects and suspected he had actually lifted all of Randall's cash.

Throwing the rope and canteen to the ground, Mattie eased down and took the items back to the cabin. Stepping in the door, he looked around and saw the two leather satchels Parker had used to carry gear and food. There wasn't much left but he managed to stuff one of them full of biscuits, a hunk of smoked bacon and a few hard beans.

Searching further, he also discovered a small amount of paper money and a few coins in the bottom of one along with a knife, fork, and some matches. He grabbed a tin plate, a cup and some medicinal papers. Then Mattie tied two long ropes around his waist and picked up the three canteens. Stepping outside, he moved around the side of the cabin and saw the rain barrels. One of them was almost empty but there was still some green-tinged water at the bottom of the other, enough to fill a canteen and a half.

A few minutes later, Mattie stepped up to the wagon where he had heaped the rest of the dried kindling and pinecones on and around the bodies. Checking the men's pockets for the last time, he found a few more coins and then—saving some for himself—sprinkled kerosene over the corpses, the kindling, and the wagon bed. He tried to think of something good to say as a eulogy but he was too hurt and weary to think of anything besides a childhood prayer he and his sister used to recite before they went to bed.

He struck a match from Parker's stash and murmured, "Now I lay me down to sleep…" When the match didn't ignite, he struck another. "I pray to God, my soul to keep," and stepped back when small, red flames streamed across the kindling onto Parker's shirtfront and over to Tulu's leather vest.

Mattie stepped away as the flames rose higher and continued, "If I should die before I wake…" Nodding in satisfaction as the fire enveloped the back of the wagon and the body of Randall Penny, he finished with, "I pray to God my soul to take."

The boy stood still for a moment watching the funeral pyre. Then he turned to follow the trampled snow and hoof prints that had carried his Marie away.

10

AMBER EYES

Snow fell in in heavy, white sheets through the trees and onto the forest floor. It gathered on branches and fell in great clumps, filling the air with crystalline explosions of frozen rainbows.

Mattie had repeatedly tumbled over stumps and fallen branches. The road he and his companions traveled just yesterday seemed like a foreign place now, hushed and malevolent. His head wound had stopped bleeding some time back but his whole body trembled and shook as if caught in a tempest.

He didn't know much about medicine but his father had talked to him once about going into "shock" and how an insignificant injury could turn fatal; he wondered if that was happening to him now. Falling again, the boy acknowledged that he was hopelessly lost.

Up seemed like down, and all sense of north and south was lost in the murky gray cloud-cover over-

head. He had meant to follow the trail back down off
the mountain and into the town with the large stockyard but that seemed as far away as the moon now. For
all Mattie knew, he had traveled in circles for the last
six hours.

His stomach cramped as hunger gnawed at his
innards despite the nausea that rose up in his throat
every few minutes. Understanding that he needed to
rest, Mattie stopped and gazed around for a few
moments, trying to get some bearing on where he was.

He saw a very tall tree with mighty branches not
too far away. Taking a deep, shuddering breath, Mattie
plunged through the snow. Thankfully, his feet did not
encounter any obstacles as he plowed his way toward
shelter. Then he stopped, gasping in fear as a horrifying sound filled the air, raising gooseflesh on his
arms and neck. A warbling, anguished howl echoed off
the trees and filled the boy's heart with dread.

Quietly moving another twelve feet toward the tree
and a clear patch of ground under its branches, Mattie
fell to his knees and let the leather sack he carried over
one shoulder fall to the ground. His head felt like a
knife had been plunged into it and his scalp burned like
fire. Mattie lifted his hands to his face and allowed
himself to weep in pain and fear. Too much had
happened and he mourned... too much death and
sorrow for one boy to endure. Unheard, his sobs filled
the air.

Finally, too weary to waste more energy crying,
Mattie dropped his hands and looked around. *I was*

lucky, he thought, as he observed the tiny clearing in which he knelt. The ground was covered in pinecones and needles. In addition, a number of dry branches littered the area...enough, perhaps, to make a small fire.

He opened the satchel and found one of the biscuits. It was as hard as old leather but—at this point —he knew he needed something in his belly, no matter the taste or texture. Then his heart skipped a beat when the hideous howling filled the air again. It sounded like nothing he had ever heard before, as if an unholy beast was roaring from the throat of hell. It sounded close, too, and Mattie could hear the sound of rushing water.

WATER! He thought with sudden hope. That was another thing his pa had once told him: "If you get lost in the woods, follow a river or a creek downstream." Mattie got to his feet, wishing the Indians hadn't taken all the guns with them when they left. Clutching a knife in his hand, he crept toward the source of the terrible howling and the sound of the water.

Stepping as lightly as he could and shaking with nerves, Mattie crested a rise and saw that a wolf struggled and snarled at the trap that held its back leg in its grip. The wolf, distracted by the boy's presence, stopped gnawing at her leg and growled. Then, whining piteously, she worked at the trap's steel jaws again.

Mattie's heart sank. Somehow, the wolf had been caught high on her leg and, as he watched, arterial blood poured out of the animal's wound. The wolf was dying right in front of his eyes and Mattie wished again that he had a weapon with which to put the creature out of its misery. He slunk from the sorry sight, aching with shame.

He knew that he was still a youngster—innocent of the world and its ways—but he had seen more cruelty and suffering in the last few months than he could believe. In all the time he had worked with Jacques Dupre', Mattie had not considered the animals that used to inhabit the skins that moved in and out of the trading post. They were inanimate, soulless rugs, hats and blankets judged by size and quality only.

Now, however, he saw the savage waste of life and the agony resulting from humanity's desire for fur. Realizing he was guilty of the same callous cruelty, Mattie vowed to do what he could in the future—if he even had a future—to keep from supporting fur trappers and traders in the world he lived in.

Stepping away, he turned to his right and walked toward the sound of a river. He came to its banks and stared down into its tumultuous, icy rapids. Growing dizzy again, his head throbbed with pain. Knowing that he needed to rest for a little while, Mattie walked back toward the tree and his meager belongings. He paused once to glance at the injured wolf and saw that the animal was resting now, her long pink tongue lying on the snow bank as she panted in agonized exhaustion.

He stumbled to his place under the tree and thought about eating another biscuit, or building a fire, or maybe following the raging water downstream into the prairies and towns below. Instead, he curled up close to Parker's old leather satchel and slept.

Mattie dreamed he was home in his bed and he smiled. It occurred to him that he must be ill. Why else would his ma put a hot-water bottle on his chest? Yes, she was wiping sweat from his face and brow and murmuring words of comfort as he tossed and turned. The boy fell unconscious again and the dream fled.

A few minutes later, however, Mattie's eyes flew open in alarm. The warm, heavy weight still lingered and his face was being scrubbed clean but he knew he was not at home. Looking up, Mattie gasped. An animal had taken up residence on his chest and the creature was licking sweat and dried blood from his cheeks and forehead.

A wolf pup with large, amber eyes was stretched out on Mattie's prone body, both paws cradling the boy's face as it licked and licked. Those beautiful eyes looked into his own and Mattie thought he saw all of eternity reflected in those golden orbs.

Then nerves took over and Mattie sat up with a cry. The little wolf tumbled backwards with a yip and landed on his back in the snow. It crept away a few feet and sat, staring remorsefully back at Mattie.

Wolf and boy regarded one another for a few moments until Mattie relented. "Come on, you..." he said, holding his hand out for the animal to sniff. He judged the puppy to be a couple months old with soft gray fur and a black mask on its face. Its oversized paws were black as well and the creature gazed up at him with a grin.

Mattie tried again. "You look like a little bandit, puppy. Come here...I'm sorry I scared you."

The wolf stared at Mattie's extended hand and back up into his eyes. Finally, it walked slowly over and licked the boy's knuckles. Content for the moment to let the pup lick his hand, Mattie realized that this animal was probably the offspring of the wolf that had been caught in the trap.

Mattie had slept soundly for quite a while. He had no way of knowing how long but, judging the failing sunlight, he figured it was going on sunset now. He could not remember hearing the injured wolf howl after he had seen her last and he wondered if she had died.

The puppy crept closer and Mattie slowly reached his hand up to caress the animal's head and ears. Whining, the baby scooted close to Mattie's thigh and lay down, trembling slightly, as the boy petted him. Then it fell asleep and, in doing so, bonded the human boy to it for the rest of its life.

Mattie sighed. His stomach ached with hunger and his head was still sore but he knew he was past the worst of his injury. The snow had lightened up as well. Tiny, white flakes flittered and Mattie could see stars winking in the darkening, purple sky.

Reaching into the pack, Mattie rummaged around and found a piece of wool rag. Taking it out, he spread it over the sleeping puppy and got to his feet. It would be dark soon and Mattie feared being alone in the forest at night. All manner of creature roamed the woods after dark; cougars and bears, perhaps even this puppy's pack mates.

Gathering dried pine needles, cones and dead bark, he cleared an area and piled everything into a pyramid. He used the last of his kerosene and, praying silently, used one of Parker's matches. There was only smoke at first, but Mattie knelt low and blew on the embers. Suddenly flames licked up and the boy added small branches and twigs to the fire.

Sitting back on his heels, he saw that the wolf pup had awoken and stared at the rising flames in fascination. Mattie thought it might be hungry or thirsty—or both—so he poured water from one of the canteens into his cup and placed it on the ground in front of the animal. The little wolf promptly drank it all.

Mattie grabbed the smoked bacon out of the oilcloth and cut a chunk of it off for the puppy. Snatching it in haste, the little wolf ran away a few feet to eat it, keeping a watchful eye on its human companion.

Mattie grinned at its greed and ate some of the meat himself along with a biscuit and some water. He watched as the pup crept back to his side, staring into the fire's depths as he stroked the puppy's soft fur.

Well, he thought, I'm alive for now. Maybe I can find my way back to that town. I have about six dollars...that should be enough to buy a bath, some food, and maybe send a telegraph to Doc Abrams...

He stood up, got a few more branches and fed fuel to the fire. Bright orange and yellow light painted the trees, sending distant shadows into stark relief. Mattie thought he glimpsed the reflection of glowing eyes watching him from the deeper depths of the surrounding forest. If so, they were close to the ground —a raccoon or possibly a beaver—and no threat to him.

The baby wolf snuggled as close to him as it could get. Feeling it shiver, Mattie reached down and carefully lifted the animal. Tucking it inside his jacket, an old one of Parker's, the wolf wriggled until it found the perfect spot, then curled up on the boy's shoulder with its nose buried in the crook of Mattie's neck.

"Don't worry, little Bandit," he whispered. "Looks like we're both on our own now so guess we'll just have to watch out for each other."

11

A TEST OF WILL

MATTIE AWOKE THE NEXT MORNING SOAKED TO THE skin. The fire was nothing but sodden ashes even though he had forced himself to rise a few times during the night to keep the flames high. He had stared into the shadows, heart in his throat, as animals lurked just out of sight. The boy shook rain out of his eyes as he remembered the night before...

Bandit had growled, the wolf's fierce snarls almost comical because of its youth. Its eyes were fierce, however, and shone golden in the fire's glow. Mattie did not doubt that the pup would attack any threat despite its diminutive size.

At one point, Mattie saw a long, tufted tail and realized the creature that threatened was a mountain lion. Somehow knowing what circled his fitful fire made things easier as he knew that panthers were timid creatures and, more importantly, loners by nature.

Standing up, Mattie grabbed a burning branch and

jerked it out of the flames. Whipping the torch back and forth, he screamed, "Get outta here, cat! Go on! Git!"

For a moment, Mattie panicked when he realized that his eyes were blinded by the light. An animal could jump him now and he wouldn't even see it coming. Then he listened carefully to the sudden silence; Bandit had stopped growling and Mattie heard no additional sounds coming from the surrounding forest.

Trembling with nerves and fatigue, Mattie rejoiced. Using the firebrand had chased off the cat so he and Bandit were safe. He picked up the wolf again, tucked it into his jacket, and slept.

...Yet now the wolf was gone and Mattie's heart sank at what might have happened to his newfound friend. As he sat gazing at the sodden fire and the plumes of misty fog enveloping the world in its clammy grasp, Mattie also understood that something was wrong with his body.

Even as he acknowledged the tightness in his chest and the raw, red burning in his throat, he started to cough. One cough turned into two and then he was overcome with a paroxysm of deep hacks that threatened to strangle him to death. As he hunched over, wheezing, Mattie felt Bandit's wet, inquisitive nose and he reached out to the animal panting anxiously by his side.

Finally, his chest stopped hitching and Mattie took a deep, gasping breath. *Shoot!* He thought. *Now I have a cold on top of everything else.*

He shivered with a sudden chill and looked around while Bandit snuffed eagerly at the satchel that held the smoked bacon. "Okay, Bandit. I know you're hungry. Let me get us something to eat," he murmured. Standing up, Mattie watched in amazement as rain-water ran in sheets off his hat and jacket.

He saw shimmering stars and heard a high-pitched whine inside his head when he bent over to open the leather sack. His stomach lurched, as well, but the wolf was scratching at the oilcloth in hunger so he quickly took the meat out and cut off a hunk. Knowing he should eat something—he actually felt his own body weight disappearing—could not compel him to partake of the meat or sodden biscuits.

Mattie let the pup have his fill while he collected his belongings. Then he called out, "Let's go, Bandit. We're getting down off this mountain… come on!"

The wolf watched as the boy moved away from the fire toward the river and then it followed. Pausing briefly by its mother's side, Bandit whined and looked up at Mattie who waited patiently, staring down at the dead wolf. Although he wasn't surprised, his heart wept with pity. The once magnificent animal looked diminished now. Nothing but skin and bones, her fur was lank with death.

"Yeah, it's a shame, Bandit, what happened to your ma." Wiping a tear from his eye, Mattie added, "My ma's gone, too."

Feeling his chest hitch again but unwilling to let

himself succumb to any more grief, Mattie turned away.

"We gotta go, son," he muttered. "I think I'm sick and I need to get both of us down off this mountain. Come!"

Bandit sniffed at his mother's corpse one last time and then bounded after the boy who followed a fairly well-defined path alongside the river. In places, Mattie had to climb and grab hold of tree roots and branches to keep on course. Most of the time, however, it was easy going.

Mattie, when he wasn't bent over grasping his knees and coughing until he thought he might puke, became more and more convinced that this was a busy trail, used by both animals and people. He saw human rubbish: an old tin coffeepot, a filthy pair of torn britches and a cast-off rag doll as he walked along.

He also saw deer scat, broken traps, and the imprint of two huge bear paws sunk into the soft, damp banks of the river. The claws on each of those prints were almost six inches long. Shaking his head and shivering with chills, Mattie backed away and called the pup that nosed avidly at the fresh tracks.

The boy walked another four hours until he was forced to stop. Swaying in place and staring up into treetops that swirled and whirled around in the sky above, Mattie had no way of knowing that he had pneumonia and that his body temperature was over 103 degrees. His teeth clacked together in his mouth and—as he fell to the ground—the wolf at his side whined, licking its new master and recoiling from his hot, fevered flesh.

Then, not knowing what else to do, Bandit crouched by Mattie's side…one orphan determined to guard another from harm.

The next few days passed in a nightmare collage of sights and sounds, all accompanied by the painful body-wracking illness that tried its hardest to kill him.

At one point, Mattie woke to the little wolf's fierce snarls. Someone—the ugliest, oldest and stinkiest man Mattie had ever seen or smelled—stood over him in the pouring rain.

Covered from head to feet in assorted furs, his long white hair was tangled and matted with mud, twigs and leaf chaff. Mattie noticed the man's gray beard sported what had to be remnants of many meals and it seemed to wriggle and writhe on the oldster's chest with a life of its own. Mattie was too weak to do much more than cry out when the man threw a tarp over Bandit.

"Don' ye worry, laddie…the wee beastie won' be harmed," the man murmured. Mattie watched as the fur-clad creature opened what turned out to be a sack, then deftly twisted it so that the wolf tumbled inside.

Mattie tried to speak yet, when he opened his mouth, nothing but deep, rasping coughs issued forth. The man shook his grizzled whiskers.

"Ack, laddie," he grunted as he scooped the boy up in his arms. "Do na try to talk…you're ill."

Mattie felt himself being lifted then placed in the

back of a wagon, watching as an invisible form lunged —growling and whining—against the sack that held it captive.

He slept, waking occasionally to gaze up at the sky with dazzled eyes. It was daytime now and clouds whizzed by in the blue sky like soldiers on the march. At some point, the old man must have loosened the ties on the sack that held Bandit as the little wolf snuffled his skin and burrowed in the crook of his neck. Mattie fell unconscious again.

He woke up to the sound of voices; he was in a dark room, his body was covered in sweat. He heard someone say, "Good, the fever has broken."

"Where am I?" Mattie croaked.

"Shh...you need to rest, son. I think you're going to lick this thing but you're not out of the woods yet. Go back to sleep." Opening eyes that seemed to be glued shut, Mattie peered up at the speaker.

Three men stood by the side of his bed. One was small and neat, wearing a checkered vest and holding a small vial of medicine to the boy's lips. Mattie obliged but cringed, gagging at the taste of the foul concoction. But the little man held his jaws closed with ruthless efficiency, forcing Mattie to swallow despite the razors lining his throat.

Lying back on the pillow in exhaustion, the boy stared up at the other two men. One was an elderly fellow with splendid white, mutton-chop whiskers. Dressed very well in a gray, silk suit and shiny black boots, he looked a little like Father Christmas only much fiercer. The thought made Mattie smile.

The man gasped and muttered, "Christ, Jon! Would you look at that? He is the spitting image of Robert..." Suddenly, fat tears were leaking out of his eyes and he fumbled for a large hanky.

Another man stepped into the lamplight and now it was Mattie's turn to gasp. At first, thinking a haint was calling, he scooted back against the wall, gasping with fear. It was his father—only taller with dark hair rather than blonde.

Lean—with high cheekbones and kind, green eyes —he stared down at Mattie and said, "I'm your uncle, Jonathon Wilcox, and this is your grandfather, Peter. We came a long way to find you, son."

Mattie looked from one face to the other and saw his father looking down at him through eyes just like his own. Then, to his shame, he was sobbing.

The doctor stood up and said, "I'll let you men talk to the boy for a few minutes but no longer than that, hear? If old Scotty hadn't stumbled across him when he did, you'd be standing by a grave instead of this sick bed. The child is not out of danger, though, so don't wear him out more than necessary." With those words, he picked up his travel kit and stepped out of the room.

Mattie lay on the bed, overwhelmed. His grandfather sat down at his side, trying to soothe his grandson with large, clumsy hands. He talked about how he and his one remaining son had packed up the family farm and come as soon as they could after hearing about what happened to Robert and his family.

"There were more problems than you can shake a stick at!" The old man exclaimed. "I honestly don't know how so many people have found their way West! Anyway, we're here now…and guess what?"

Mattie shook his head as his grandfather stared down at him with joy. "We found little Maudie! She is just fine and settling into our new home in Spokane."

Mattie opened his mouth but no words came. Thinking back on what had happened since his ma and pa died, and seeing his little sister packed up and hauled off to parts unknown, had set Mattie's soul adrift on an unfamiliar sea.

Even now, as he gazed back and forth at the two familiar strangers, he felt alone and lost without a friend in the world except…"Bandit, where's…"

"So that's what you call this tough, little customer," Jon murmured.

Mattie's uncle had left the room for a moment but he stepped back in leading the baby wolf on a long, fine rope. The pup stared up at Mattie, gave one excited bark, and leapt onto the bed.

The two travel-weary but triumphant men stood by the bed and watched Mattie bury his nose in the wolf's soft fur. Sobs wracked the boy's frail shoulders, but a smile was etched across his face.

Robert Wilcox's twin gazed down at his nephew. He saw how thin and sick the boy was but his brother's physical beauty was reflected in those large green eyes, long straight nose, and wide finely-etched lips.

Praying to heaven one last time for his dead sibling, Jonathon vowed to do everything in his power to make his brother's son as safe and secure as he possibly could.

PART II

THIRTEEN YEARS LATER, AND KNEE DEEP IN A PIG WALLOW

MATTHEW TOOK off his hat and hung it on a post, then removed his vest and placed it on the ground next to his gun belt. Rolling up his shirtsleeves, he observed his quarry with narrowed eyes.

"Sure you want to do this, Boss?" Matthew's deputy, Bob Higgins, couldn't help but feel a little sorry for what was about to happen to Clancy Jones once Sheriff Wilcox got his hands on him. *Rules was rules though,* Bob thought, and Clancy had broken one of the sheriff's cardinal rules when he beat his wife and kids senseless after drinking it up at the saloon last night.

"It's alright, Bob," Matthew murmured. "This is going to be fun."

Climbing the split-rail fence, he leaped into the pigpen screaming like an angry Indian. The sty housed about thirty hogs, big and small, and shit was knee-deep but Matthew plowed through the brown muck as if he was strolling through a field of daisies. Clancy, who had tried to escape the sheriff's wrath by jumping into the pen, backed up with terror in his bloodshot eyes.

Meanwhile, Bob, Evan and Murray—Matthew's three deputies—whooped and hollered, laughing while some of Granville's good citizens drawn to the ruckus collected impromptu wagers on the brawl's outcome.

"Now, now, Sheriff," Clancy pleaded. "Calm down, son, afore someone gets hurt…EEEEE!"

"Whoa, that's gotta smart a bit, I reckon." Bob grinned as Matthew launched his body in the air and drove Clancy straight down under the ocean of mud. Hogs squealed and snorted and one old sow lunged at Clancy's boot that waved enticingly in the air as he fought against Matthew's grasp. The sheriff turned around, shooed the pig away, then hauled Jones up and shook him like a terrier with a rat.

Normally a kind and soft-spoken man, Matthew could not abide a bully. "If I EVER hear about you hitting your wife and kids again, EVER…," he snarled, "I will cut you up in little pieces and feed you to these swine!"

Clancy squirmed and squealed almost as loud as the pigs. "No, Mattie! I won't do it never again, I swear!"

More violent shaking and Matthew growled, "What did you call me?"

Clancy groaned and whimpered, "Uh…oh! Sheriff! Yeah, I'm sorry, Mat…I mean, Sheriff Wilcox…Sir!"

He hurled Jones down in the mud again with a splash and said, "Don't you forget it either!"

Matthew sauntered back toward his deputies as Clancy wept in the hogwash. Although the young sheriff was slick and brown with filth from hair to heels, the way he carried himself spoke of a grace not often seen in these parts. Shoulders back and head held high, Matthew signaled to Evan and Murray with a grin, then stood still as they tossed a bucket of water at him, washing most of the muck away.

"Hold on for one more dousing!" Murray laughed and scooted back to a nearby horse trough. Turning around, the sheriff lit a cheroot and waited for the water to clean his backside.

"Ready, sir?" Evan inquired. Although twice as old as his boss, Evan held the young man in respectful and almost superstitious awe.

"Hold on a minute," Matthew said. "Here, Bob. Keep this dry for me, will you?"

Bob took the lit stogie and stepped away with a grin as the water splashed over the sheriff's back and legs. Clancy was getting the same treatment from his family on the other side of the pen.

Finally, soaking wet but dignity intact, Matthew said, "You boys head on back to the jailhouse. Make sure the prisoners are fed and, Bob, be sure to fetch the minister to the jail so those boys can hear the word of God before Saturday, okay?"

Bob's smile fell flat but he nodded in obedience. Once every three months or so, the circuit judge came to town. For the most part, Judge Watkins was lenient but, occasionally, a "bad" outlaw was imprisoned here. Although Watkins was not considered a hanging judge, he also did not believe in tarrying once he tapped his gavel. Last week, he had come through and announced his judgment upon a train robber and a horse thief. Since there was a loss of life during the perpetration of both crimes, these two men would hang.

Matthew continued, "My uncle is coming to town today. Evan, would you please light the woodstove in the shack so Jon and I can talk privately?"

The shack was actually a lean-to that Matthew had built snugged up next to the jailhouse. It had two windows and contained a small couch, a table and two chairs, and the stove. This was the place the sheriff took visitors and assorted dignitaries. It was a private place away from prying ears and eyes, removed from the prisoners whose fate was decided by their peers.

Evan donned his hat and said, "Sure thing, Boss."

He and Murray walked away as Bob said, "I guess I'll go talk to the preacher then, Matthew. Where will you be if we need you?"

Matthew grinned and said, "Taking a bath!"

Whistling to Bandit—his friend and companion who had stayed on an abandoned porch across the street away from the smelly pigpen and his master's antics—Matthew walked up the dirt road toward Madame Chang's bathhouse. He walked quickly but many citizens called out greetings as he went by. Most of them grinned at the sight of him and the wolf although a couple of kids held their noses, smirking, until Matthew roared and threatened to chase after them.

He stopped for a moment and watched as the widow Imes stepped down off her wagon and waited on the boardwalk for her two children to climb off from the back. As always, his heart skipped a beat when he saw her coppery-red hair, large amber eyes, and ginger freckles that dusted her creamy skin. Although she was tall and lean, her breasts stretched the fabric of her dress and Matthew's knees went weak with longing.

Iris Imes saw the young sheriff gazing at her and she turned away quickly so he could not see the tremors that shook her limbs or the blush staining her cheeks red. "Blast that boy!" she murmured under her breath. It wasn't as though she hadn't given him enough encouragement, after all. It was two years now since her husband had been killed in a rockslide and a year since she had put away her widow's weeds.

Four months ago, she had danced with Matthew at the Mayor's Ball and the heat between them almost cast sparks in the air to the amusement of the gossips in town. Then, just last month, she and her children were the last ones in the sleigh when over two feet of snow stranded Iris's neighbor, Betsy Williams, as she went into labor.

Matthew had fetched the doc from town and

brought him to Betsy's house in the blizzard and, later, took Iris and her children home. Sending the kids inside, Iris reached over and took Matthew's hand. "Won't you come in?" she had asked as bold as brass.

The sheriff held her hand for a moment and looked deep into her eyes. Then he sighed and shook his head. "I…can't. I'm sorry, Iris, but I just can't."

Iris took a deep breath. "Well, you let me know when you can, Matthew. I'm not getting any younger, though…" Dashing a tear out of her eye, she gathered up what was left of her dignity and scrambled down from the sleigh.

Although Iris still dreamed of the beautiful young sheriff, she would not embarrass herself again. She nodded at him now with cool detachment and herded her kids ahead of her into the mercantile.

Matthew sighed and continued down the street. He knew he had hurt Iris and sometimes wished he could just put his memories away in a box and never chance upon them again. However, another girl's image haunted him, one with black hair and blue eyes. Marie…

In the twelve years since Matthew Wilcox had been kidnapped and almost died from pneumonia, he often dreamed of finding Marie, rescuing her and getting revenge upon the outlaw known as Top Hat. Yet, when rescued by his beloved uncle and grandfather, it was all Matthew could do to regain his health.

Pneumonia turned into scarlet fever and, for months, the boy was confined to his sick bed in his grandfather's opulent home. Mattie might have gone crazy with boredom but Peter and Jonathon wasted no time in furthering his education. Tutor after tutor came in to teach Matthew everything from arithmetic to Latin, the art of warfare, and the beauty of poetry.

Maude often joined her brother and soon they re-established their bond, becoming friends as well. Finally, Matthew regained his health and was allowed outside. He played, rode horses, and learned to shoot his uncle's rifles and pistols.

Jonathon had been a captain in the confederate army during the War of Northern Aggression, but now he yearned for peace and quiet. He was a pragmatist, however, and knew that pacifist leanings were just wishful dreams, especially in the rough, unsettled Northwest Territories. He became a sheriff and helped keep order in the booming new city of Spokane.

However, he did not intend to let his nephew and foster son go untrained into the unruly landscape. So he set to teaching Matthew everything he knew about defending himself and others from hostile intentions. The boy was taught gunplay, sword work and hand-to-hand combat; he was also taught animal husbandry, smithy work, and how to sew.

When he wasn't training with his Uncle Jon, Matthew read the law with his grandfather, Peter. He learned how to manage the family's wealth and studied the finer art of politics and governance. Matthew actually hated these lessons but he smiled through them because he adored his grandfather and uncle equally and would do anything to please them.

When Peter passed away soon after Matthew's twenty-third birthday, Jonathon took over his father's law office as an attorney and Matthew stepped into his uncle's shoes as a sheriff. He took the place of Marty Wiscomb in Granville—a smaller township just outside of Spokane's city limits—while Marty took Jonathon's place.

Now, two years later, Matthew hurried into the bathhouse to wash up and put on clean clothes. He had not seen or talked to his uncle in over a month and was anxious to once again clasp Jonathon's hand in love and friendship.

13

A CHANCE AT JUSTICE

A FEW HOURS LATER, MATTHEW SAT AT HIS DESK IN THE jailhouse going through paperwork and listening to the Presbyterian minister speak to the two condemned men. Pastor Cook was a young fellow with a kindly manner and he sat on a straight-back chair in front of the adjacent cells. The sheriff could not hear what was being said to the prisoners but he saw that both men were studying the pastor's face as if the secrets of the universe were written on his countenance.

Matthew's deputy, Bob Higgins, was cooking venison stew across the room and the other two deputies were outside fixing broken tack and brushing down the sheriff department's horses. Then he heard a wagon pull up and cries of welcome...his Uncle Jon had arrived.

Standing up and walking outside, Matthew greeted his foster father with affection. "Why don't we go into the shack?" he said.

Jon, who had admired his nephew's idea of a separate meeting room, had ordered a similar structure built next to his own jail. Nodding in agreement, he said, "Let me use the facilities first, nephew. I'll just be a minute."

As Jon moved around back to the outhouse, Matthew went inside to get coffee and food but Bob was ahead of him. Holding a tray with two bowls of stew, a loaf of bread, spoons and cups, he grinned at his boss and said, "Got you covered, sir!"

"You sure do," Matthew replied. "Thanks...let's head in."

They stepped into Matthew's private sanctuary; the room was warm and inviting and the young sheriff gazed around with pride while Bob set the refreshments on the table. "There you go, Sheriff. Call if you need anything else," he said and walked out the door just as Jon entered.

Bandit got up from his place close to the woodstove and lifted his muzzle to smell the stew. Matthew put a small amount of his own dinner down on a plate and watched, smiling, as the wolf gobbled up the warm meat and vegetables. Then Bandit turned and wagged his tail at his master's foster-father.

There were two people in the world that the wolf loved with all his heart: Matthew and Jonathon. He grinned as the older man bent down to scratch his ears and then curled up on his blanket again.

Taking off his hat, Jonathon smiled and said, "You run a tight ship, son."

Smiling, Matthew said, "Learned it from you, Uncle. Sit down, please. Bob made us lunch."

The two men sat and ate while exchanging news about the family, local politics, budget cuts, and the latest criminal cases in and around the Spokane area. Jon informed Matthew that his sister Maude—who had married a wealthy cattle rancher—was expecting her second child. They made tentative plans to ride the train to the Ellensburg area for a visit.

On a sour note, it sounded like Ronald Whittaker, a Union sympathizer from New York, was on the fast track to be elected mayor. This was bad news for the local sheriffs as it was well known that Whittaker was as tight as a tick with municipal funds.

Finally, Jonathon pushed his bowl to the side and opened his leather satchel. It was time to talk about the job and, for some reason, Matthew's uncle suddenly looked old and worn out. He was over fifty now and his hair carried more salt than pepper, but there was something gray and tired in his uncle's normally youthful carriage.

Jonathon took a stack of papers out of the satchel and placed them neatly on the table. Matthew noticed that his uncle placed one of the papers upside down and out of the way of the other stack.

Looking up, Jonathon asked, "Mind if I have another cup of that coffee, son?"

Shaking his head, Matthew said," Of course not, Uncle. Help yourself...there are some cookies there, too. Little Maggie from the bakery brought them down today when she heard you were coming." Matthew watched his uncle pour a cup of coffee and consider the cookies before walking back to the table.

Jonathon smiled as he sat down and said, "You give that gal a hug and a kiss for me, Mattie."

Now Matthew was beginning to worry. Usually his uncle was a no-nonsense, taciturn man who was not the type to use nicknames or lavish affection on others, not to mention the fact that Jonathon had not called him Mattie since he was fourteen years old.

"Uncle, is there something wrong?" Matthew inquired.

Jonathon looked at the young man he thought of as a son and smiled again. Dodging the question, he asked, "I'm fine, son, just fine. But what about you? When are you going to settle down and make an honest woman out of one of these gals in town?"

Matthew felt his cheeks warm. I'm only twenty-five, for pity's sake! He thought defensively. Why are folks always trying to hitch me to the marriage wagon?

He stared his uncle in the eye and said, "There's plenty of time, sir. Right now, though, I have things to do."

Jonathon nodded. "Of course you do, Matthew. You're new at this job and the county election is just next year. You will win it though, of course. The people in this town love you and won't let you get away easy. What else is stopping you?"

Matthew squirmed, uncomfortable under the weight of his uncle's regard. He knew that in order to

move on with his life he had to try to find Marie and—
if possible—bring his old enemy, Top Hat, to justice. He
was embarrassed now to think that he had allowed
himself to be lulled into a state of calm complacency.
He was embarrassed and filled with shame that he was
letting Marie down.

In addition, Matthew hadn't heard a thing about his
old nemesis in over five years. Randall Penny's cousin
could be anywhere by now and, although wanted
posters had circulated as regular as clockwork for a
while during Matthew's adolescence, it had been at
least four years since the man had either died or went
to ground.

*Still, he thought, I can't move on until I find out what
happened to Marie and Top Hat.*

Jonathon studied his nephew's face and sighed. He
knew exactly what tormented the young man and
drove him away from hearth, home and the love of a
good woman. It was guilt, plain and simple, and a
massive sense of duty to the ghosts of his past.
Knowing he was possessed of the same personality
quirks, Jonathon tried a different tack.

"I heard that the widow Imes was seen on Whittak-
er's arm two weeks ago at the spring dance in Spokane
Falls." He smiled as his nephew's green eyes widened.
He added, "I think she is a sweet thing, don't you, son?"

Looking away, Jonathon added, "Margaret tells me
that a number of boys are showing up at the Imes farm
lately. A woman like that—beautiful and well-to-do…
well, they don't grow on trees…"

Matthew thought about his uncle's wife and frowned. Marge was the sweetest woman in the world but she was also the town's biggest gossip and match-maker. She was the one who had urged him to dance with Iris at the Mayor's Ball in the first place and he still hadn't gotten over that experience.

Swallowing his displeasure at the thought of that weasel, Whittaker, putting his sweaty paws on Iris's body, he asked, "Shouldn't we be talking about work, Uncle?"

Jonathon grinned, knowing he had gotten the boy's goat, but complied. Turning a number of posters over, Matthew started taking note of the outlaws displayed on paper and wrote down how much money each arrest would earn his office. There were logistics to consider, like the time and distance the sheriff and his deputies would need to travel, the food and supplies needed for the chase, and how much firepower the outlaws possessed. All these factors weighed against the bounty on each criminal's head.

Jonathon's experience as sheriff had placed him in a unique position as the current District Attorney for Spokane County...a position both Matthew and his counterpart, Marty Wiscomb, were grateful for. Jonathon was able to peruse the newest wanted posters and determine, through wisdom and experience, the most likely candidates for each assignment. He would consider manpower, funds available and the fighting capabilities of each sheriff and then divvy up the crimi-nals, accordingly.

He also had a knack of getting his hands on reports of the worst—and, therefore, the most highly sought after and rewarded—criminals, long before anyone else in power even saw them, including bounty hunters who seemed to have an underground network all their own.

Finally, when the men had gone through the small stack of posters and split up the duties between the two sheriff's offices, Matthew sat and stared at the one remaining which was face down on the table. Nodding at it, Matthew asked, "So, what are you hiding from me, Jonathon?"

He was half-joking but his uncle's reaction was not funny. The man sat up straight and glared, "Mattie, if it was up to me, I would never show you this face at all."

Matthew sat up as well and the hair on the back of his neck prickled. Suddenly, he knew what was hidden from his eyes. He reached over, grabbed the poster and drew it close. His uncle made a half-hearted attempt to snatch it back but gave up with a grunt of resignation. Standing, Jonathon walked over to the woodstove for one final cup of strong black coffee.

Bandit, sensing his master's tension, arose from his bed and went to Matthew who sat reading the poster. The wolf whined once and nosed the young man's arm in anxiety but was ignored. Sitting down, the animal's piercing eyes studied Matthew's face as he finally spoke.

"How long have you had this, Uncle?" Mattie's

voice, as always, was respectful but anger simmered under his words.

"Not long, son…it came in a couple of days ago. I figured it could wait until I came to visit."

"I have been waiting for years, Jonathon!" Matthew exclaimed. "There could be a hundred bounty hunters hot on Top Hat's trail by now!"

"There might be a few, son, but not that many yet. Remember, so far, only my eyes have seen this," Jonathon responded.

Matthew jumped up, his chair creaking noisily across the wooden floorboards. "Sir, I would like to resign my position as sheriff and go after this snake!"

With a soft growl, Bandit stood as well. Glancing back and forth at the two men he loved, he whined anxiously in confusion.

Jonathon looked at his foster son with sorrow. "Did you read the whole thing, Mattie?" he asked. "The man is called Razor Head now. I hear it's because he likes to slit the throats of the men and women he rapes!" The big man paced in agitation. "Not to mention that he has a whole gang backing him! They call themselves the Mad Hatters after some fairy tale book." He paused and took a breath. "Each and every one of those men is the worst kind of criminal…and they are all murderers, every one of them."

Matthew just stood there, lips set and green eyes as hard and cold as emeralds. There was a tension-filled silence in the room and Jonathon's shoulders slumped in defeat. He had lost the battle of wills yet he knew that Matthew would have eventually found out and left —with or without—his family's blessing. At least this way, Jon could do something to help…give money maybe, or extra firepower, swift horses, anything!

His eyes filled with tears of loss and fear for the boy he loved. Silently, he nodded and opened his arms for an embrace. Matthew hesitated a moment, studying his uncle's eyes, and then stepped into the hug. Jonathon held his son for a moment and prayed that he had taught the boy enough to survive the contest.

14

POSSE

Two days later, Matthew, Bob, and another Spokane Falls deputy named Roy Smithers mounted their horses in the early dawn. They were equipped with three additional horses, one mule, extra firearms, ammunition, grub and arrest warrants.

Jon had done everything in his power to enable his foster son's safe return, including moving his law office into Matthew's shack and taking over the duties of Granville's sheriff while Matthew was gone. Evan McCauley and Murray Kotes were put out that they were told to stay behind but Jon needed their support...besides, they were both too old to undertake the task.

Jon studied the three men on horseback and sighed. These men were far too young yet there was no stopping them. Matthew—Jon's son for all intents and purposes—was only twenty-five years old and Bob was barely out of his teens. Roy Smithers, though, was a little older than the others at twenty-nine and Jon hoped that the family man, who had a wife and three sons at home, would temper the two hotheads in the upcoming conflict.

"Sir," Matthew said, startling Jon out of his worries. "I just wanted to thank you again for all your help. I never expected such a smartly outfitted posse."

Nodding, Jon said, "All I want is for you to come home in one piece. That means, go about this the smart way. Try to pick 'em off one by one. Do not go after the whole gang at once, you hear me?" He glared up at them.

"Yes sir," they answered in unison.

"Good," Jon replied. "Now remember, every chance you get, I want you to report in. The gang is mainly holed up in the North Idaho territories although I heard that a couple of those skunks like to party in the saloons around Kellogg and Wallace…lots of gold and silver there." He took off his hat and scratched at his thinning gray hair.

"Also, you will pick up some tag-a-longs on the way and I want you to make them welcome. The Mad Hatter gang has killed a lot of good people around that area, folks who made an honest living from mining precious metals. So…" Jon stared his nephew in the eye. "You are not the only man with an ax to grind, son."

Matthew looked down at the pommel of his saddle

in consternation. He *did* resent the fact that their posse was going to grow larger—thus slower and more cumbersome—the closer he got to the gang. He hadn't really given much consideration, however, to all the other people whose lives were ruined by the man he knew as Top Hat.

Nodding, he said, "You're right, Uncle. We will make the other posse members feel at home."

"We sure will, sir," Bob agreed with a grin.

Jon sighed. The daylight made Bob Higgins look about thirteen years old with his long, wavy brown hair, freckles and puckish smile. The boy had not stopped grinning since he was informed he would accompany his friend and idol, Matthew, along on the scout.

Feeling Mr. Skeleton tickle his breastbone, Jon scowled and said, "Well, Bob, you stay sharp and listen to what these older, wiser men tell you. Just because you can shoot a running jackrabbit between the ears doesn't mean that you can stop a bad outlaw who is out to kill you. I don't want to see any of you coming home in a box!"

Bob's eyes got big and round. He was unaccustomed to seeing Jon Wilcox mad and wished he had kept his big mouth shut. But since the old man was still staring at him with scary-looking eyes, he mumbled, "Yessir, I will."

Matthew nudged his horse forward and held out his hand for a shake; Jon reached up and said, "You keep me in the loop, son."

He started to reply but his foster father had already turned away and stepped onto the porch with Evan and Murray. Bandit paced nervously back and forth, nipping at the heavy rope holding his body captive and whining as he stared at his master. Usually the wolf went everywhere Matthew did but he didn't want to worry about the animal this time out.

Glancing around, Matthew noticed a few other citizens had awoken early and come out to pay their respects. There was Dish, the blacksmith, and Maggie, the baker's daughter. The town doctor, Tim Dearbourne, was there too, along with Pastor Cook. They all looked at the posse with solemn expressions on their faces, as if mentally saying goodbye. It sent chills up Matthew's spine.

"Hup-Hup!" Roy clicked his teeth and brought his horse up to a trot. Matthew and Bob waved at the small crowd as they followed Roy with the pack mule and extra horses in tow. They heard the town folk cry, "Goodbye, boys! Give 'em hell!" and "You come back safe now!"

Soon, they were out of town and headed east toward Idaho Territory.

They had ridden about five miles when Matthew saw a plume of dust rising up from an adjacent road to his right. He stopped his horse and took out his monocular but then he spied a spectacular roan pulling a buggy. The woman driving the fancy carriage snapped her whip in the air above the horse's backside

and her long, copper-penny hair sailed behind her in
the bright, sunlit morning.

"Here comes the widow Imes, Matthew," Bob said.

"When are you going to do something about her?"
Roy drawled. "I've been hearing about this thwarted
love affair clear into Spokane Falls lately."

Iris had rounded the corner onto the main road and
pulled her mare into a trot as they approached. Usually
the woman wore her hair in a sedate bun and her skirt
and waistcoats were modest, buttoned up tight and
designed to cover every square inch of her arms
and bosom.

This morning, however, it looked like she had
stepped into her skirt while still wearing her night-
gown. Matthew saw tiny pearl buttons and lace
peeking out from under her oilskin coat. Her bootlaces
were untied and her hair hung down past her hips in
fiery disarray. Her brown eyes and pale, freckled skin
seemed to shine with a light of their own as she stared
at Matthew from the buggy's seat.

"Holy shitfire!" Roy breathed. "No wonder every
buckaroo from Canada to Montana is in the courtin'
game these days. What in the hell is the matter with
you, Matthew?"

He glared at the man but turned to watch as the
carriage skidded to a stop in front of them. Iris climbed
down and stood in the road, staring up at Matthew.

"May I have a word with you, Sheriff?" she asked.

Matthew's heart suddenly thundered in his chest.
He had admired Iris from afar for many years and

thought she was pretty in a proper, mature sort of way. But now he understood that this was a twenty-seven-year-old woman in her prime, full of energy and sexy beyond belief. Dismounting, he took off his hat and walked up to her.

Her eyes snapped with anger. "Did you really mean to ride off without a fare-thee-well?"

Behind them, Roy smirked and young Bob Higgins blushed. "I sure am glad that lady ain't mad at me," Roy muttered. "She looks like a regular hellcat."

Meanwhile, Matthew studied the ground at his feet. He *had* meant to send word to the widow Imes via his Aunt Margie, but time had slipped away from him in the mad race to find Top Hat before a bounty hunter got to the outlaw first. He looked up and saw that her beautiful eyes were brimming with tears. It seemed he had hurt her again.

He opened his mouth to apologize but she said, "Oh, shut up." Then she took a step toward him, wrapped her arms around his shoulders and kissed him on the mouth.

It was no chaste peck goodbye as Iris poured every ounce of passion she possessed into her kiss. Her tongue explored Matthew's lips and her body pressed up against his with sensual intimacy. It was if she knew how well they would fit together...like two puzzle pieces meant to join as one.

Although the sheriff knew his deputies were watching his every move with barely restrained hilarity, he couldn't help but return the kiss. His body responded to Iris from head to toe, including a more unruly part of his anatomy. Cheeks flushed with desire, Matthew allowed the embrace to continue for a few more moments and then he stepped away.

Iris stood in front of him and reached up one hand to put pressure on the place where her heart resided. Her chest heaved with longing, her cheeks flushed red. Her eyes, however, were filled with sorrow and Matthew could see she was struggling to find composure.

Finally, she whispered, "Well, young man. Look me up when...and IF...you find your way back home." She walked back to her buggy, jumped in and yelled, "Ha!" to her showy mare. The horse took a little hop then responded to its master's steady pressure on the reins, pulling the buggy in a loop on the road before heading back the way it came and down the access road leading to the Imes's farm.

Matthew slapped his hat against his thigh for a moment as he watched Iris's retreat. Mounting his gelding, he ignored his deputy's loaded silence and knowing glances. Then he growled, "Let's head out!"

Jon had stepped into the jailhouse to do some paperwork and prepare for the hanging that would take place in two days. Evan McCauley and Murray Kotes were gone, looking into the reported theft of four sheep from the Martinez farm.

Bandit sat still, studying the wooden shutter that took the place of a glass window in the back of Matthew's business shack. There was a long dowel driven through the latch that kept the shutter closed and the wolf stood up on his two back legs to get a closer look. Large, golden eyes took in the security measure and the animal bared his long, white teeth...then he placed those fangs on the dowel and pulled.

15

BULLIES

THE POSSE MADE GOOD TIME AND DECIDED TO STOP FOR the night next to a large river. They could see a town in the distance and Matthew realized they were close to the settlement of Schee-Chu-Umish. Named after a fierce tribe of Indians known as sharp traders, the French called them Hearts of Awls...Coeur D'Alene. Sadly, many of those natives had been pursued by military forces and eventually subdued, making room for the ever increasing influx of white settlers.

The sun was just starting to set in the crook of two low-lying mountains and the sky was lavender in the falling dusk. Matthew stretched his long legs and took a brush out of his saddlebags. Lifting the saddle and blanket off his gelding, the sheriff brushed the horse and picked some burrs out if its tail as it fed on green shoots of wild grass by the riverbank.

His two deputies followed suit and, for a moment, Matthew felt peace descend upon his heart; a peace he had rarely experienced since his father died on the dusty streets of Pinckney City, leaving his family destitute and alone. As always, those memories filled his heart with grief and troubled his thoughts with a yearning for revenge.

If it wasn't for Randall Penny and his cousin Top Hat, Matthew thought, things might have gone differently for me. I could have been happy with the Dupre' family and, by now, Marie probably would have presented me with many fine children.

However, Top Hat had killed the Dupre's and Matthew's own dreams the day he rode in to the trading post to steal what was not his. Good mood in tatters, he lightly slapped his horse's rump and let the gelding wander un-hobbled for a while before darkness settled in.

Grabbing a metal pot and three cups out of his bags, Matthew walked down to the river to fetch water for coffee. That's when he heard the sound of voices raised in excitement and the startled, frightened cries of someone being struck. He stood still for a moment, listening, and then he walked over to where his pistol, a Colt-Paterson five-shot, was tucked into his bedroll.

His two deputies picked up their guns as well, stiffening in alarm when they realized that the screams they heard were feminine. Someone out there in the deepening dusk was setting to in a harsh manner with their womenfolk and both men knew that was something the sheriff would not abide.

They joined Matthew where he stood staring up at

the slope of a small hill. "We'll stalk up there real quiet..." he whispered. "Bob, you go that way." He pointed right. "And, Roy, you go left and loop around. We'll take a look but you two don't do anything until I say so."

Bent over in a crouch, the three men ran up the hill and lay on their bellies at the crest, looking down. It was hard to see what was actually happening because of the failing light, but Matthew lifted a spyglass to his eye and observed the activities in the small clearing below them. Gritting his teeth against the rage rising in his chest, he made a conscious effort to calm his breathing.

Six U.S. soldiers were holding a small band of Indians captive. The natives were bound to one another with metal wrist cuffs and a long iron chain. They were seated together on the opposite side of a bonfire though it was obvious that a few of the female prisoners had been freed.

The soldiers, all of whom appeared to be falling-down drunk, surrounded the women. They were cavorting around, taunting and laughing, while their fellow soldiers were taking turns raping the females.

Matthew's mouth sagged open in shock as he realized that many of the women appeared to be quite elderly with wrinkles, frail bones and long, white hair. As if rape was not bad enough, the soldiers hit, bit and kicked the women when they finished.

Looking past the awful sight—while trying in vain to keep his fury in check—Matthew studied the

Indians who were tied up and watching helplessly from the other side of the fire; they were old men and a few young boys. The boys shouted in anger but the old men just wept silent tears.

Matthew saw his deputies approach slowly, creeping low and steady on either side of him. Looking to his right, he whispered, "Come on over, Bob...you too, Roy."

Settling down in the grass beside the sheriff, Roy muttered, "Sorry business, Boss. What should we do?"

Matthew sighed and said, "What we SHOULD do is walk away and forget we ever saw this..."

Bob gasped. "But sir, we gotta help..."

Matthew laid a hand on the young man's shoulder. "Shhh! I said that is what we should do...it is never a good idea to go up against the U.S. Army. There are too many ramifications and too much paperwork involved." He lifted the spyglass to his eye again and winced as a woman cried out when a soldier mounted a little girl.

"However," he growled, "we are going to stop this, right now! I need both of you to swear witness if this goes to a court of law...do you swear?"

Both Bob and Roy nodded vehemently and then they made their plans.

About a half hour later, three men crept down the hillside into the small valley. Like ghosts, they came out of the dark from three directions at once. The soldiers —caught up in their drunken, lustful frenzy—did not notice the new arrivals but many of the Indian men and women did.

The captives silently watched as the tallest, a handsome man with a silver star pinned to the crown of his hat, took the hilt of his knife and cuffed one of the soldiers on the back of the head, rendering him prostrate and unconscious; the other men did the same thing with two more of the soldiers. Within seconds, they were trussed up in a heap.

The three soldiers still in the act of rape suddenly realized that something had changed and stopped their sexual assaults. Looking around in bewilderment, they jumped up in alarm and stared at their friends.

The three ghosts had melted into the shadows and the Indian captives could not help but smile, knowing the remaining soldiers did not stand a chance against the men with stars on their hats and chests.

"What's going on? Who's out there?" one of the soldiers yelled, staring with superstitious awe even as he fumbled at the buttons of his pants. Then, like a wraith, the tall man reappeared and hit the man a heavy blow to his head. The soldier sagged to the ground, his flaccid penis still exposed. There were two other soldiers left, however, and one of them seemed far more sober and quick on his feet than the others.

The Indians saw him bend and pluck a pistol from a leather belt, taking aim at their saviors; one shouted a warning but it faded to silence as a huge wolf sprang out of nowhere and latched its teeth onto the soldier's wrist. The man let out a squeal of rage and fear as he fell, the snarling animal on top of him.

The Indians did not understand what the tall, golden man cried but the wolf stopped its attack immediately and ran to him, grinning and wagging its tail with joy. The Indians knew a powerful totem when they saw one and they murmured to one another in amazement.

In confused panic, the two remaining soldiers tried to escape but the men with stars on their chests grabbed and beat them, quickly tying them to the rest. Then the saviors started writing words on paper in very large letters. None of the Indians spoke the white man's language so they did not know that RAPISTS was written on the signs. They did understand, though, when the golden-haired man rummaged around and found a set of keys in one of the soldier's bags.

He walked over to where the Indians sat chained together and put the key in an iron padlock. Within seconds, the chain slithered loose from their wrist cuffs and then the man took a different key, snapping each of the cuffs open.

Many of the soldiers were awake by now and hollering in rage but the three men paid no attention. Instead, they wrapped shawls and blankets around the women and shooed them toward their tribe members who stared and wondered what to do. Then the tall man made a familiar gesture with his arms and said, "GO! Go on, hurry!"

The Indians quickly faded into the night.

"You're gonna pay for this!" one of the soldiers hissed as Matthew and his deputies wrapped the same long chain around them.

The two deputies kept silent but the man with the sheriff's star answered, "Is that right? Last I heard rape is still a crime punishable by firing squad, if you're a soldier and by hanging, if you are a civilian."

Finished with the prisoners, Bob and Roy stepped away and watched their leader who stared down at the soldiers in fury.

"They was just a bunch of filthy Injuns!" another man cried. "Are you really gonna leave us here?"

"Yes," Matthew said. "However, we will inform the closest sheriff. I'll let them decide what to do with you." Slapping his hat against his thigh, Matthew spat on the ground at their feet. Then he turned to Bob and Roy. "Let's get the hell out of here. The reek of these so-called soldiers is making me sick."

The three men walked away to the sound of the soldier's pleas for mercy and understanding. Reaching camp, they then loaded up and made for town.

16

A RECKONING FOR TWO SKUNKS

THE SHERIFF AND HIS TWO DEPUTIES RODE INTO TOWN... such as it was. A haphazard sprinkling of canvas tents, old covered wagons and vendor's carts squatted in mud a foot deep in places. There were two wooden buildings; one appeared to be a saloon and the other was a mercantile. The mercantile was closed up tight but the saloon was filled to overflowing, rambunctious with tinny music and drunken shouts of glee.

Sighing, Matthew got down off his horse and said, "Guess there are no hotels around here." He hitched his horse to the rail in front of the saloon thinking that a deputy must be around somewhere.

Panting, Bandit ran to him and Matthew took a long rope, tied the wolf to a post on the boardwalk in front of the building, and told him to stay. Turning to his men, the sheriff said, "I don't mind if you boys want to wet your whistle. It's been a long day. Only one, though, okay?"

Bob and Roy nodded. The younger deputy untied a wooden bucket from the mule and said, "I'm going to give these horses some water from that trough. Then I'll be in."

Matthew smiled and said, "Thank you. We won't tarry so come in quick if you want a drink. I'm just gonna ask if there's a boarding house around here."

He and Roy entered the saloon and stood inside the large room, looking around. There were loggers and miners, trappers and card handlers. At least a dozen prostitutes circulated, looking like a flock of exotic birds in their bright silk dresses and red lips. They looked well-fed and reasonably happy which meant the owner was taking care of his investments so Matthew relaxed a little. Walking over to the bartender, Matthew ordered two whiskies and asked if there was a boarding house or a sheriff in town.

The heavyset man studied Matthew's star, then placed the drinks in front of his new customers. Pursing his lips, he let a long line of spit drizzle through his front teeth and said, "The sheriff and his deputies are in town…about three miles yonder. This is just an outpost."

When his lips twisted in a sneer, Matthew thought he was going to have trouble on his hands but the bartender said, "I'm the owner of this establishment… name's Monroe." He stretched his hand over the bar to shake. Frowning he continued, "Deputies step in here once a night but mostly they stay clear on account of those rascals over there." He pointed toward the back of the room where four men were playing cards.

Matthew took note of the fact that most of the women steered clear of that table and many of the men, as well. Looking closer, he saw that two of the players looked familiar. His heartbeat sped up a little and he leaned over to whisper in Roy's ear. "Don't look that way but I think we got us a couple of fish. Let's study those warrants."

Monroe hustled off to fill a few customer orders and then came back their way. Picking up a long, white rag, he polished some glasses in front of them and said, "Those boys come in here once a month or so. I think they are with some outfit or other and by that I mean the Mad Hatters. They've roughed up my girls and stolen from me."

Watching the two lawmen as they shuffled through the paperwork, he leaned over and whispered, "Yeah, that one. He's the worst of the bunch." Stepping back, Monroe added, "I wish you could take care of those ruffians for me…"

"Terrence Delaney," Roy mumbled. "Wanted for robbery and murder. Reward of one hundred dollars," he read aloud. Turning to Matthew, he hissed, "This is a good one. You want to try it?"

The sheriff was studying the room's reflection in a grimy, marbled mirror above the bar. He was just about to answer his deputy when he saw all four of the men at the table stand up at once.

"Watch out, Roy," he murmured and turned around,

pulling his pistol free of its holster. Then Matthew shouted, "You there, Terrance Delaney! Stand still and put your hands in the air!"

The noise in the saloon stopped and Matthew heard a few muffled cries as many of the patrons slid off their chairs and hustled under their tables. But his heart sank when he heard the terrified screech of a young woman. Delaney, who was the furthest away, had grabbed one of the whores and now held her pressed up against his chest with a bowie knife across her jugular.

The other three men were edging away but froze in place when Matthew spread his feet wide apart, leveling his pistol at Delany's head. The girl's eyes were huge as she stared down the octagonal barrel of death aimed in her direction.

"You can do one of two things right now, Delaney," Matthew spoke quietly. "You can let that girl go and come with us where you will be tried by a jury of your peers or…" The sheriff took a step forward and closed one eye, staring down the barrel of his gun with the other. "I will shoot you dead where you stand."

Roy cocked his rifle with a loud, snapping rattle and customers scrambled out the front door with squeals of fright. Bandit, suddenly startled, began to growl and snarl on the porch. Then Bob came running in with his deputy's star in full view. Like an angel, he was briefly illuminated by the lamplight inside the saloon before one of the outlaws pulled a hidden pistol out of his coat pocket and shot him in the chest.

"No!" Matthew screamed and shot Delaney in the face; Roy's rifle boomed and chaos ensued. The remaining patrons fled as Matthew stepped over to the man he had shot and nodded in satisfaction. Delaney was dead and so was another of his partners in crime but two of the outlaws had made their escape in the riot.

As Roy helped the young whore who was shaking with nerves and covered in blood, Matthew ran quickly to where Bob lay on the wooden planks. The boy's eyes were open and he said, "Sheriff, I'm alright. I think he just winged me."

"Shhh, let me see," Matthew whispered and gently peeled the boy's coat away from the wound. He didn't realize he was holding his breath until it rushed out of his lungs in relief. Bob was right; it was only a flesh wound although a good five inches of skin was torn open in a long, bloody furrow a couple of inches deep.

"Somebody get me a clean cloth and fetch a doctor...NOW!" Matthew roared.

"I'm sorry, sir..." Bob murmured, his cheeks pale with pain and worry.

Matthew smiled at his young deputy and said, "You have nothing to be sorry about, Bob. If anything, this is my fault." Shaking his head, the sheriff said, "You are correct, though. This wound of yours will not kill you but you will be down for a while. I'm sorry, too."

Bob's eyes filled with tears and Matthew understood they were not tears of pain, but of frustration and disappointment.

Monroe ran up and handed Matthew a small pile of clean rags which he carefully pressed to the boy's wound. Then Bandit was by his side, whining anxiously.

"Good Lord, Bandit. Can't you ever behave?" Matthew whispered softly as the wolf nudged at Bob's arm.

Then he heard hoof beats and shouting outside, followed by two men angrily calling for peace and quiet. Looking up, Matthew saw a skinny, middle-aged man staring down at where he sat on the floor next to Bob. Bandit snarled at the expression on the man's face.

"What is the meaning of this?" the newcomer demanded.

Matthew sighed and cursed himself for a fool. He was not kidding when he told Bob that he, himself, was to blame for the fiasco. He realized now that his blood was boiling and had been since he first took off on this mission. He was consumed with rage and the need for justice…so much so he had made two potentially fatal mistakes on their first day out: freeing the Indian hostages, then trying to make an arrest in a crowded bar.

He understood that he would need to make an account of his actions to the town's acting sheriff or he and his men might be detained until his Uncle Jon sorted things out. A small kernel of cold fury in his soul burned bright with righteousness but the cooler part of his intellect informed him that, if he didn't slow down and start thinking things through, he might just get himself and his posse killed. He was about to stand and introduce himself to the other sheriff when a half-dressed man scurried through the doors, reeking of whiskey and livid at being rousted out of bed. Yet he was tender enough when he fell to his knees and started treating Bob's wounds.

Matthew stood up and showed his star to the sheriff. Then he stuck his hand out and introduced himself. "My name is Matthew Wilcox, sir, and these are my deputies, Roy and Bob."

The man stared up at him and his hostile expression faded. "O'Brian is my name and this here is Sam Winston. What in blazes are you doing in this shithole, Sheriff?"

Matthew saw the hurt expression on Monroe's face, but gritted his teeth and smiled. "We were coming in to make your acquaintance but mistook this outpost for a town in the dark. Then we saw Delaney sitting back there and decided to serve our warrants on him and his buddy." Hating to do it, he nevertheless swallowed his pride and said, "I see now, I made a mistake. You have my apologies, Sheriff O'Brian."

O'Brian studied the young man's face and nodded. "Well. What's done is done, I reckon." Staring down at the dead bodies of the two outlaws, he continued, "At least these two skunks won't be bothering people around these parts anymore."

Looking at Matthew and Roy, he said, "Let's head on into town. It's only three or four miles from here and we can set you up with some warm grub and rooms at the local hotel." O'Brian gazed at Bob and asked the doctor, "Jones, is that boy fit to travel?"

The doctor shrugged. "This wound is not life-threatening but I don't think he should try jumping on a horse quite yet. How about I send him down later in the buggy after I stitch him up?"

O'Brian turned to Matthew with his eyebrows raised. Matthew nodded and said, "Roy, you stay behind with Bob and make sure he makes it into town safe."

Roy replied, "Sure thing, Boss."

O'Brian's deputy and three other men were hauling the two dead outlaws out the front doors by their feet. The skinny sheriff shook his head and sighed. "There's gonna be hell to pay for this, you know."

Matthew frowned and asked why.

"Well, the leader of this particular outfit has a tendency to take an eye for an eye, especially when it comes to his men." O'Brian walked over to an empty table, picked up a half-full glass of whiskey, and swallowed it in one gulp. "And to make matters worse, the Army boys down at the fort are up in arms. Seems that six of their soldiers are missing."

17

TOP HAT: THE PERVERTED TWISTS
AND TURNS OF A PSYCHOTIC MIND

THE NEXT MORNING—AS MATTHEW FACED THE WRATH of the fort's commanding officer, tried to comfort Bob who tossed and turned with feverish agony from his wound, and snuck away to send a telegraph to his Uncle Jon—a rider left town and headed east into the higher, piney hills.

Sam Winston worked two jobs: one as a deputy for the Coeur d' Alene sheriff and the other as runner and roustabout for Kevin Walker, aka Top Hat or—more recently—Razor Head. By far, the one Walker offered paid the most.

Winston had once been an honest man but, when his wife got tuberculosis, he knew he needed more income to pay for her medicine and the opium that kept her comfortable. She was a little better now, although when he was home he hated to hear her rattling rails and see the bloody hankies staring up at him from wherever she let them fall.

In addition, Louise had not given him sexual relief since she first grew ill four years earlier. Lord knew he had tried but a man has needs. So when he started fulfilling those needs at the bosom of a certain whore named Little Jeanie—a tongue-in-cheek reference to the size of her enormous breasts—Sam grew more and more convinced that his wife was a burden he no longer wanted to carry.

He told Jeanie once that he wanted to carry her off and move back to New Orleans and the devil take the hind-most. She studied his face carefully for a moment and then informed him that she had no intention of trading a sure thing for a life with a poor man... married or not.

This frustrated Sam to no end. He had lots of money but most of it was hidden. After all, how could he explain his sudden wealth? The small town had very big ears and the gossips loved nothing more than to wag their tongues at each other at the slightest whiff of scandal. So he hoarded his ill-begotten wealth, played the part of a law-abiding deputy and tolerated the wife he had come to despise.

Now, as he rode toward the Mad Hatters' hideout, he thought about the rich reward he was about to receive. He would tell Top Hat about the Spokane County sheriff named Matthew Wilcox; he would also inform the crew that Delaney and Skeeter were laid low by this same sheriff and his deputy.

He grinned, thinking, this might just be my big payday! If Top Hat pays me enough, I'll throw caution to the wind and tell Jeanie about the money I have stashed. Maybe then she will agree to leave town with me and start up fresh in Louisiana.

Sam entered the encampment a couple of hours later. The lookouts were tense and surly; apparently, word had already arrived that Delaney and Skeeter were dead. He greeted the gang members and made his way to Top Hat's tent.

The boss was inside, surrounded by his most trusted men: Ike Nelson, his second-in-command; and Chollo Gonzales, one of his best shooters. As always, when he spent one-on-one time with the gang's leader, Sam's palms grew slick with nervous sweat. He had heard too many stories about the man's past deeds to take him lightly.

"Hi, Boss," Sam said carefully.

Sharpening his bowie knife, Top Hat stared up at him from his chair in the back of the tent. His long mustache covered most of his crooked, bucked teeth but his eyes were what struck fear into Sam's soul. They were close together and small, glittering with hate. Those brown orbs looked straight into a man's gullet and made a fellow feel very small.

"So" Top Hat said in his girlish, high-pitched voice, "what happened last night?

Sam felt a stealthy finger of fear run its clammy touch up and down his back. *Is the boss mad at me?* He wondered, nervously clearing his throat.

"Well, I was doing my rounds and this Spokane County sheriff rode into town with a couple of his deputies. Before I knew what was happening, that same sheriff—a kid by the name of Matthew Wilcox—was serving a warrant on Delaney and then all hell broke loose."

Now the sweat ran freely down Sam's nose as Top Hat's eyes grew wide when the sheriff's name was mentioned. The boss sprang to his feet and paced back and forth a few times, twice taking agitated swipes at his own possessions with the knife as he walked by. Then Top Hat took two long steps in Sam's direction and placed the edge of the weapon against Winston's throat.

"Why didn't you come in last night and let us know what was going on, huh?" Top Hat hissed. "Why is it that we had to hear about it from Tommy and Edward?"

Sam swallowed, feeling the edge of the razor sharp knife nick his neck. "Boss, O'Brian asked me to settle the sheriff and his posse into the local boarding house. Also, I had to take the youngest one, the one that Tommy shot, to Doc Jones' place to get sewn up and then on into town. I got here as soon as I could break away, I swear!"

Top Hat's sour breath filled Sam's nostrils and he thought he saw something dark slither across the man's pupils. Then he knew no more, except for the fact that he was on the ground and couldn't breathe. He had a moment to realize his throat had been slit and that he was a dead man before he closed his eyes forever.

Top Hat stared down at Sam Winston's body with a

half-smile on his face and then he frowned. "Shouldn't have done that, I reckon," he murmured.

The other men looked between their boss and the murdered deputy. Chollo didn't care in the slightest that the deputy was dead. He was just annoyed that the tips of his boots were getting soaked with blood. Ike, however, glared in resentment.

Sam Winston had been the source of invaluable information for the last three years. He was the first to inform the gang when a rich stagecoach was scheduled to arrive in the area, or a barge loaded with furs and cash was due to sail up to the docks on the big lake. Winston was also instrumental in securing their best payroll ever when he told Top Hat that a group of wealthy industrialists was coming to the area to make an investment on the new rail system being built in the Spokane Falls area.

Now that valuable source was nothing but a pile of offal on the floor. He leaned over and spat in disgust, making sure he spit on the dead body so the boss would assume his disgust was aimed at the two-timing deputy.

Top Hat walked over to his chair and sat down. "Sorry about that, boys, but Winston was becoming a loose cannon," he stated softly. "We do have trouble on our hands, though…"

"Why's that, Boss?" Ike asked.

Top Hat scratched his ears for a moment, then replied, "That sheriff, Matthew Wilcox, I know him.

We've had dealings together in the past and I reckon he's out for revenge."

"What happened?" Chollo wanted to know.

"That's none of your fuckin' beeswax, that's what happened." Suddenly, Top Hat was pacing across the floor again swishing at thin air with his bloody knife. He was muttering imprecations under his breath and stabbing at some invisible foe.

Both Ike and Chollo knew better than to test Top Hat's temper. They stayed as still as possible, letting their boss rant and rave until he finally sat down again with a sigh.

"Thing is," he muttered, "if that boy is wearing a star now like Winston claimed, then he is going to be a peck of trouble. He could appeal to the territorial legislation for funds and gather as big a posse as he needs to hunt us down." He glared at both men in turn.

"So do you see why we need to be sly about this?" he asked. "Before now, O'Brian was appeased by a little payoff here and there. Plus, we had Winston for info…" He paused, staring down at the dead body at his feet. "Goddamn it! I shouldn't have lost my temper!" he exclaimed.

Both men looked away, careful to neither agree nor disagree with Top Hat's words.

"But now there is a Washington Territory sheriff hunting us down," he snarled. He studied Chollo's scarred face, his black braids, and the silver Conchos that studded his boots and belt. Then he turned to Ike who could dress proper if he had a mind to do so.

"I have a plan, though." Top Hat's little brown eyes jittered in their sockets as they always did when he got excited. "Ike, I want you to head into town and dress nice so you don't scare the folks there. I want to find out where Matthew Wilcox calls home. Who his people are and anything else that gives us an edge." He grinned with malevolent glee.

"Meanwhile, I'm going to send a bunch of the boys east to wreak havoc on the surrounding countryside. That way, while Sheriff Wilcox is looking for us there, we three will circle around and pay a little visit on the sheriff's hometown."

18

A RESCUE MISSION ABORTED

While the Mad Hatters buried Sam Winston deep in the ground then started packing up their camp in order to move further east into the mountains, Matthew Wilcox sat facing Bob Higgins on a straight-backed chair. He was shaking his head as the young man pleaded his case.

"But, Boss...I'm good to go, see?" he said as beads of sweat popped up on his face.

Matthew sighed. Bob would be fine—eventually—but, right now, he was not fit to travel much less participate in a posse. His left shoulder was a mass of red, purple and blue-black bruises. The bullet that had plowed through the young man's shoulder cut a deep ridge in the muscles and weakened his left arm so much he could hardly raise his hand despite Bob's efforts to prove otherwise.

"Stop that, Bob! Right now!" Matthew said.

Bob groaned and let the pistol in his hand drop

onto the mattress. He was still weary with pain and wasn't even aware of the tear that ran like an errant child down his cheek. Looking up at Matthew, he asked, "Can't I talk you out of this, sir?"

Matthew replied, "I'm sorry, Bob, but no. Jon has already sent a buggy to come and pick you up. Don't think for a minute that Roy and I won't miss you but Jon said he could use your help back home. As much as you are able, I want you to help my uncle out with paperwork and the like until we get back. Okay?"

Roy stepped in and spoke to the young man as well. "Yeah. But you're a game rooster, that's for sure."

Bob stared back and forth between the two men and then he lay back down on the bed. "I reckon you're right." He sighed. "Don't know if I could heave that LeMat gun up in the air if we got in a pinch."

Jon Wilcox had provided the posse with two 42-caliber, LeMat revolvers, a unique black ball pistol with secondary, smooth bore barrels capable of firing buck-shot like a shotgun. Bob had never seen such a thing and he had been itching to try one out. Instead, he was heading back home.

Matthew smiled and said, "Well, we aren't leaving quite yet and I'll be back to see you off when the buggy gets here." He added, "You are still my number one deputy, Bob. Roy and I will see you soon."

Turning to Bandit who had risen from an old fur on the floor when his master stood up, he said, "Bandit, you stay with Bob, you hear? Stay!"

Roy leaned down and gave the younger man a

playful tap on his right shoulder and then both men stepped outside into the fresh air. Off in the distance, snow-topped mountains loomed; closer, the beautiful waters of Lake Coeur d'Alene sparkled in the sun. The town was bustling with soldiers, traders, miners and business owners of every stripe.

Matthew knew the real reason for the town's growth spurt: GOLD! There were at least a half a dozen gold and silver mines within a 50-mile radius of this settlement so it was no surprise that a strong criminal element had taken up residence as well.

The main road into town was fairly well-maintained despite the mud and, even as Matthew watched, he saw a group of men on a wagon stop about fifty feet down the road. They unloaded a pallet of fresh-cut lumber, buckets of nails, and started working on a new boardwalk.

The town's sheriff, Mellon O'Brian, walked up and said, "How's young Bob doing this morning?"

"He will recover, sir. Thanks for asking," Matthew replied politely. "Have you heard anything from your deputy yet?"

The previous evening—while he, Matthew and Roy ate dinner in one of the better restaurants in town—O'Brian had confessed that his deputy was missing.

"That man has had a tough go of it lately," he said. "His wife Irene took ill a few years back and I think he's going broke keeping the poor gal in medicine. I always thought that Sam had a faraway look in his eyes...you know, the kind of look a man gets when he's fixin' to take off." O'Brian heaved a sigh and reached into his back pocket for a handkerchief.

"I know he's got family down in Louisiana, I think." Frowning, he added, "Just seems strange that he left without saying goodbye."

"What about his wife?" Matthew inquired.

"Oh, Mrs. Winston should be alright. Our church folk will take her in, fer sure. Besides, the doc says she don't have much time left before she needs to go to the hospital anyway. Sam did a pretty good job keeping her alive this long but her days are numbered."

Now, as the sheriff frowned into the early morning sunlight, he said, "I haven't heard nothing yet. I suspect he up and left but, just in case, I am sending a couple of men out to look for him. You know how things go sometimes…a horse can spook on you, or a high-wayman will decide to take all you have." He looked down at his boots adding, "I just want to make sure before I give him up as gone."

Matthew kicked a pebble off the boardwalk. "Any word yet on the deputies who want to join my posse?"

O'Brian brightened. "Oh yeah, I almost forgot! I just got word that a couple of men from the Silver Valley area are headed this way. I figure they'll be here by late tonight or tomorrow morning."

Matthew nodded. "That's good, Sheriff. Roy and I are anxious to be on our way."

O'Brian scratched a spot under his hat and asked, "When do you figure that buggy of your uncle's is due to arrive?"

Matthew thought for a moment and replied, "Probably not until late afternoon. Why?"

"Well, Winston was probably my best deputy. He had experience and some pretty good tracking skills. My other two boys are willing but maybe not so able, if you know what I mean. So I was wondering if you would consider giving them a hand in looking for Sam for a few hours. I would be sure that your young deputy has some company and I would also be obliged to take your help as trade for the doctor's bills."

Matthew gazed at Roy and when the deputy nodded in the affirmative, he turned back to O'Brian. "That would be fine, Sheriff. Roy and I both have some skill at tracking."

"That's great!" O'Brian smiled. "I told my boys to be ready by ten o'clock." Consulting his pocket watch, he said, "That's in just under an hour. Can you be ready to go by then?"

"Sure, we'll be ready. Have your deputies meet us here."

O'Brian walked away down the boardwalk. Turning to Roy, Matthew said, "Let's get a quick bite to eat before we fetch the horses."

As Matthew and Roy headed to one of the town's two restaurants, Colonel Le'Bouff and a number of his soldiers trotted by from the opposite direction. Matthew tipped his hat but the colonel just glared.

Matthew was forced to endure the man's fury the day before when he confessed that it was him and his two deputies who trussed up the soldiers and adorned them with signage for all to see. Luckily for the soldiers, no one but Le'Bouff's men saw the word RAPISTS on the white sheets of paper but it was a narrow escape as dawn was breaking when the commander's troops liberated the captives and brought them back to the fort.

According to Le'Bouff, however, each Indian delivered to the reservation earned the fort a bounty of ten dollars. Since those bounties had disappeared into the night, he figured that Sheriff Wilcox owed him $150.00. Matthew was loath to do it but he had asked his uncle to send the required cash along with the buggy.

Yet, apparently, Colonel Le'Bouff was now entertaining doubts about whether the cash was on its way or not. Grinning, Matthew turned to Roy and murmured, "Guess that commander is still pissed at us."

"Fuck 'em," Roy replied.

They stepped into a small wooden building and sat down at a long bench astride two barrels. A cheery, middle-aged woman turned away from her cook stove and blew a sweaty lock of hair off her forehead.

"Howdy, boys!" she said. "We have biscuits and gravy this morning...or beans and bacon. What'll it be?"

They both ordered biscuits and sat back to wait for their breakfast to arrive.

There were a couple of men and women in the restaurant. One man looked to be hung over; bleary-eyed, he winced at every loud noise. The two women were obviously prostitutes. Their heavy eye makeup and rouged cheeks looked garish in the stark sunlight streaming through the establishment's one window but they giggled companionably as they studied the local newspaper.

Another man sat quietly and stared at them openly like he was familiar with who they were. He was tall with long, gray hair and wore an old, shiny suit though his vest and boots were new. Matthew nodded his head courteously and then turned to Roy.

"Did you happen to get a look at Sam Winston's horse last night?" he asked.

Roy shook his head. "I did but, to be honest, I'm not sure if it was a gelding or a mare. But it was a big piebald...I saw that much."

"Okay," Matthew said. "That gives us something to work with anyway." He looked up and smiled his thanks as the cook served them two plates piled high with biscuits and steaming hot sausage gravy.

The men started eating their breakfast and then they heard the fellow with the handsome vest say, "Excuse me, but I couldn't help but overhear your conversation."

Matthew set down his fork and wiped his mouth with his napkin. Raising his eyebrows, he said, "Can we help you with something?"

Ike Nelson shook his head. "No," he replied. "But I thought maybe I could help you...name's Clarence Dodson." He stood up and walked over to shake hands.

The sheriff and his deputy stood and introduced themselves, then sat down to their meal again.

"Anyway," Ike continued, "the reason I butted in on your meal was on account of hearing you were looking for a big piebald mare. Well, I saw one just this morning as I rode into town...kind of hard to miss such an ugly hoss!" Matthew and Roy watched as the man laughed at his own joke.

"Did that horse have a rider?" Matthew asked.

"Sure. Skinny guy...face like an old hound dog? He was heading west when I saw him. He was loaded up, too, like he was in for a long haul."

Ike watched as the two lawmen exchanged a glance, then decided he had done all he could to divert attention away from Winston's real whereabouts. He also decided to have his boss, Top Hat, shoot that piebald as soon as possible. It was too damned showy and, if seen, would draw the attention of the two hard-faced men now sitting in front of him.

Backing away, he said, "I hope that helps. It's a big country and I figure it's my Christian duty to help a sheriff out anytime I can." Tipping his hat, Ike bowed a little and walked out of the restaurant.

Roy said, "Well, I see no sense in wasting O'Brian's time by searching for a runaway deputy, do you?"

Matthew was silent for a moment, thinking. It sounded like Sam Winston had done just what O'Brian thought he did... skedaddled away from his sick wife and headed back home to Louisiana. But something smelled off to him and he didn't know what.

The man known as Clarence Dodson seemed, at first blush, like a humble man...a peddler maybe, or a traveling preacher. His eyes, however, told a different story. Those gray orbs were as cold as gun iron and seemed to slither away from direct contact like a snake in tall grass.

Then again, as he'd said, it was a big country full of beasts—human and animal alike—and a man needed to be tough and, at least, a little cold to survive it.

Finally, Matthew nodded. "I agree. We'll tell Sheriff O'Brian what Dodson said and let him decide."

19

A FOX IN THE HENHOUSE

"Do I know you?" O'Brian stared at Ike Nelson in confusion.

Ike smiled. The last time he had clapped eyes on Sheriff O'Brian was five years ago after he and a few boys shook down a wagon train just outside of Orofino. Nelson knew his face was covered with a large kerchief then and his gray hair was brown, so he didn't think there was any way the sheriff could recall his face.

"Nah," he said. "I've never been here before. I guess I just have one of those faces. Actually, I've just arrived from the D.C. area. The President made me and a few other fellas justices of the peace and sent us out to serve papers in some of these wilder territories. Like I said, my name is Clarence Dodson. Pleased to make your acquaintance." Ike took a step forward, extending his hand to shake.

O'Brian smiled and clasped the man's hand. "Well,

God knows we need a few more justices around these parts. Are you planning on serving papers around here?"

Ike shook his head. "No, but there have been some disputes further east. And Yankee and Confederate sympathizers are fixing to start a whole new war up here and I've been sent to help divide the territories so the guilty parties can't get their hands on each other."

O'Brian's eyes got big as this was news to him. Clearing his throat he said, "Gawd damn, Idaho just got its territorial rights. What in blazes is going to happen now?"

Ike grinned and said, "Don't you worry none, Sheriff. Looks like you won't be losing any territory; it's just being shifted around a bit to help separate those groups. I don't have the particulars yet but, from what I understand, nothing is going to change in this neck of the woods.

Actually, Ike Nelson had kept a close eye on political maneuverings in Washington, D.C. He figured the only way a fellow like him could stay safe was if he had enough information to keep one step ahead of the powers-that-be. He had fled his hometown in Georgia before the war when he heard that Union troops were heading that way as he had no intention of being conscripted to fight or letting the war effort seize his property.

Through careful research, Ike also knew which routes were safest from Indian attack, and where some of the richest wagon trains and coaches were located. He knew where railroad tracks were being laid and studied up on when and where the richest gold mines were. Those places had proven to be a veritable "goldmine" of easy money for a man like him.

Now, standing up and moving to the window in Sheriff O'Brian's jailhouse, Ike stared outside and said, "I ran into a young sheriff and his deputy this morning at that little restaurant down the street. I heard them talking about a posse to hunt down a fella by the name of Winston."

O'Brian nodded. "Yessir, they were. But that search has been called off. Seems like someone..." O'Brian stuttered to a stop and added, "Well, they must have been talking about you. They told me a man saw Winston heading west on a piebald this morning."

Ike nodded. "Yup, that was me alright. I coulda been wrong but you don't see that kind of horse every day. Hope I was right to mention it?"

"Oh, yes." O'Brian nodded. "I've got a limited budget as it is. Finding out that my man skedaddled like I thought saved me a lot of money so you have my thanks."

Ike smiled and murmured, "You are welcome, Sheriff." Then he frowned thoughtfully and asked, "Mr. O'Brian, I was admiring that other young sheriff in town...the pretty boy? Is he one of yours?"

"Nope. That young man is out of Granville, a small town about twenty-five miles southwest of Spokane Falls. He took over the star when his uncle, Jonathon

Wilcox, retired from sheriffing and started practicing law."

"Is Granville where the uncle practices law?" Ike's heart swelled with relief. Looked like he had gotten all the intelligence his boss wanted in one stop.

'Well, not normally," O'Brian said. "Wilcox is the district attorney in Spokane Falls but he took over sheriff duties in Granville when his nephew took up the posse."

"What's that posse after anyhow?" Ike asked.

O'Brian scratched his head and sighed. "You're not from around these parts so you wouldn't have heard of them. But there is a bad bunch of outlaws here who go by the name of the Mad Hatters."

"Oh?" Ike exclaimed.

"Yup," O'Brian answered. "About half of them carry a pretty high warrant...one hundred to five hundred dollars reward money per arrest. I figure that young Matthew Wilcox is after some of that bounty money to boost his coffers."

"Ah..." Ike murmured. He had found through his years of banditry that young, ambitious sheriffs often staked their reputation on how much money they could raise while in office. Some of the most successful sheriffs and rangers in the country were wealthy with bounty money and shared that wealth with the local citizens. He tended to avoid those lawmen and their towns religiously.

O'Brian grimaced, adding, "I woulda done it myself but this place is growing too damn fast for me and my boys to go chasin' off after a bunch of highwaymen. Besides, usually when those crooks do get too close to home, I find some money in the form of damages sent my way to make up for the loss. I don't like to take the cash but I gotta do whatever it takes to keep this town healthy."

Nelson was careful not to let his pride show. It had been *his* idea to buy off the Coeur d' Alene sheriff in the first place and he was gratified now to hear that his plan had kept the gang safe for as long as it had.

O'Brian stood up and said, "Well, I see that a carriage just rolled in. I think that might be the buggy Jon Wilcox sent to pick up one of his deputies who got shot last night. I best get going."

Ike Nelson stood as well and smiled. He was once a fine-looking young man who had set feminine hearts aflutter all up and down the Mississippi River in his cardsharping days. Some of that charm remained and, when he extended his hand to shake a final farewell, O'Brian had no idea he had just been seduced and robbed of vital information by Top Hat's right-hand man.

O'Brian said. "I wish you a safe journey into the Dakotas, Mr. Dodson. And be careful. The Nez Perce and Blackfoot are pretty riled up. If you stay on the main road, though, you should make out okay."

The sheriff and the outlaw shook hands a final time and then Ike Nelson stepped outside to get one last look at the gang's quarry.

Jon Wilcox stared at Higgins as he swayed in

Matthew's arms. Bandit whined in worry and kept close to the young man as he was helped into the buggy.

"Get up, Bandit...Up! Up!" Matthew said. The wolf jumped in the buggy and sat down next to Bob.

Matthew slammed the door shut and, looking in at Bob as Bandit anxiously licked his face, he said, "You heal up fast. I'll be home before you know it. And make sure this wolf doesn't come chasing after me this time, okay?"

"Yes, sir, I will. See you soon!" Bob replied then let his head fall back on the seat.

Matthew walked over to where Jonathon stood next to Mallon O'Brian. "Thank you, Uncle Jon. I really didn't expect you to come all this way but I know Bob appreciates the kindness."

"It was my pleasure, son," Jon said. "Here's your money to pay off that crooked colonel." The older man handed over a small wad of bills, which Matthew tucked in his vest.

Thanking his uncle again, Matthew said, "I guess there are two deputies riding in from the east. They should be here by tonight." Turning to Roy, he said, "Give Jon the warrants on those two rascals we got last night. They should fetch a hundred dollars apiece. Maybe that can go to paying you off and the doctor here in town."

"Yep," Jon answered. "This will help." Looking around at the bustling community, he added, "Maybe I ought to move my practice over here. I heard that folks were finding a lot of gold and silver around these parts but I didn't realize how many people had come to the jubilee."

O'Brian exclaimed, "We could use another attorney in town, Mr. Wilcox."

Matthew nodded, smiling. "Yeah, an attorney might just make himself rich living here and then he would need to pay a bodyguard a handsome wage for protection."

Jon stared at his foster son and marveled anew. His brother had been a handsome cuss and Matthew carried his pa's bone structure and muscle strength along with his mama's golden hair and green eyes. No wonder half the young ladies in Granville were coming in on a daily basis to inquire after the whereabouts of their handsome young sheriff.

Jon grinned. "And I take it you're volunteering to be my bodyguard?"

"Sure thing, Uncle. Roy and I both volunteer for the job...if we could ever pry you out of Spokane Falls, which I doubt." Matthew chuckled along with the other men.

Jon nodded. "Yeah, reckon you'll bury me there when I'm done with life's duties."

A herd of low-flying clouds suddenly darkened the bright afternoon sunshine and a gust of wind rattled the tin plating on the doctor's roof. Hearing thunder grumble in the distance, Jon tipped his hat and said, "Looks like a storm is blowing in. I would rather be home by my fire this evening than stuck out in a tempest, so I will say goodbye and get on my way."

Matthew's hat flew off and tumbled down the boardwalk a few feet. Chasing after it, he snagged it by the rim and screwed it tightly on his head. He was just about to turn around and wish his uncle farewell when he noticed Clarence Dodson mount his horse about a hundred feet down the road. The man's cherry- red roan did a little crow hop and Matthew saw the twinkle of Mexican Conchos scattered here and there on the saddle.

Interesting hardware for a salesman, Matthew mused, and then tipped his hat at Dodson's friendly wave. Shivering a little in the cool and gloomy wind, Matthew shook his uncle's hand and watched as he took off for home.

20

A SORRY SIGHT TO SEE

MATTHEW AND ROY WERE JUST SITTING DOWN TO dinner when three men stepped inside the restaurant, looked around, then approached their table. Although they were damp from the rain that had started up earlier and their boots were filthy with mud, it was obvious to Matthew that the newest members of his posse had arrived.

Standing up, he smiled and held out his hand. "You must be the deputies in from Wallace and Worley."

"Yes, sir. My name is Travis Hitchcock from Worley," an older man said. "And these two are from Wallace." Pointing to the men behind him, he added, "Earl Eggars and Hoss Jenkins."

The two men smiled and shook hands as Matthew introduced Roy Smithers. "Pull up a stump and eat something...Henrietta makes some pretty good chuck,"

Roy said as the three deputies hung their dripping coats on pegs by the front door.

"I heard that," Henrietta cried. "Venison stew and sourdough for dinner, boys…want some?"

The heavyset woman had been in front of her stove since dawn and yet she still carried a smile for everyone who walked into her restaurant. Of the two eateries in town, this one was by far Matthew's favorite. Although plain with its rough plank floors and oilskin curtains, Henrietta kept it as clean as possible, warm with laughter, and filled with simple but tasty food.

The fancy place across the street with its white tablecloths and crystal chandeliers carried the cloying stench of high society. Technically, Matthew and his family *were* high society if money was the measure of such stuff and nonsense. But he had never felt comfortable with the gaudy trappings of wealth.

Matthew and Jon both lived simple lives, although Jon's wife Margie had tried to gild the lily a few times over the years. Both men knew how to use their cutlery in a pinch—and dance a waltz if necessary—but they were most at home in simple company and with plain folk.

"Yes, ma'am, thank you," Travis said and sat down at the table as the two other men pulled up chairs. Sheriff Wilcox and his new posse ate dinner and talked long into the evening about how to go about chasing down Top Hat's gang.

"You know," Travis said, "it's hard sometimes

figuring out who the outlaws are around here. You got your mine bosses who ride herd on those miners something fierce and, to my mind, some of those turds should spend the rest of their lives in jail. Then you got your Pinkertons. They like to act civilized but, in truth, some of those men are scarier than the outlaws they claim to be hunting down."

He gave a disgusted sigh and finished off the last bite of huckleberry pie on his plate. "And the criminals themselves, hell…" he continued. "Some of those boys are so rich they just sell the law off to the highest bidder. Shoot, Deadwood is a good example. That town is run by crooks and no lawman in his right mind wants to go afoul of the power in that place."

Matthew had listened to Travis Hitchcock for over a half hour and taken many notes on the man's viewpoints which seemed sensible and well thought-out. However, there was a strange note of shame underlying the man's words that made Matthew uncomfortable.

Deciding to deal with the problem directly, he said, "I wonder, do you know where Top Hat and his boys are now?"

Travis nodded. "Yeah, mostly, although the whole bunch of them seems to be on the move further east lately. Something has got 'em riled up." The middle-aged man stared into Matthew's eyes.

"Son, all of us are very aware of where those boys are, all of the time. We have to be…they are the worst bunch of crooks we have ever had the displeasure to lay eyes on." Turning to Jenkins, he said, "You tell him, Hoss."

Hoss was a heavy man in his mid-thirties with sun-chapped skin and kindly blue eyes. Looking over at Matthew, he said, "Sheriff Wilcox, with all due respect, I can see you are itching to go nab these scoundrels just as fast as you can get your hands on them. Am I right?"

Matthew could feel a hint of censure coming his way, but what Hoss said was true. "Yes," he agreed. "I have a history with the leader of that gang and I want to grab as many of those boys as possible before every bounty hunter in three territories show up and beat us to the punch."

The big deputy nodded. "We all want that, sir," he replied. "Problem is, most of us have just been trying to stay the hell out of the way and keep our people safe." His face had turned an alarming rose color and he mopped a large, white kerchief over his sweating brow.

"It's one thing when you're dealing with a regular ruffian or a simple bandit, but the Mad Hatters are a different breed, Sheriff." Hoss was leaning over the table now, eyes boring into Matthew's face.

"I have come across things those boys have done that made me lose my breakfast, sir. They have raped women, young girls—and boys, by God—then slit their throats for the sheer fun of it," he hissed. "There is no rhyme or reason for it either. There have been survivors who told me that, although the victims gave up all their worldly goods without complaint, Razor

Head goes all hog-wild and kills them anyway!" He sat back in his chair, chest heaving with anxiety.

Travis patted the younger man on the back and murmured, "Calm down, son." Then he turned to Matthew.

"The same goes for me and Earl here, Sheriff. God knows we have tried and we have nabbed a few of them, too. But taking the whole bunch down is a hard proposition. Every time our sheriffs step up to put an end to things, we suffer for it. They have burned whole farms and towns; they have hung innocent men up in trees to serve as a warning. I'm sorry, Sheriff, but I can see in your eyes you think we are cowards and we are not."

Matthew stared across at the three men who gazed back at him in shame and defiance. He suddenly realized that he had indeed been acting about half-disgusted with the lot of them and he felt like an arrogant pup, self-important and naïve.

He dipped his head and murmured, "No. I am the one who is sorry...for your losses and for my attitude. But that changes now." Turning to Roy, he added, "My deputy and I welcome your company and all the advice you have to share.

Matthew saw Henrietta close the front door to the restaurant and turn a sign on the window that read CLOSED. Looking down at his pocket watch, he said, "It's getting late, boys. If we're going to head out first thing in the morning, we should all get some shut-eye, don't you think?"

Nodding and yawning, the five men stood up, thanked the restaurant owner, and trooped outside to the local boarding house to catch some sleep. Matthew was the last one out the door and he fished in his pocket for a moment, finally finding a ten-dollar bill. Handing it to Henrietta, he said, "Thank you, ma'am, for your fine food and good service."

Her eyes got big and she said, "Son, that is way too much money!" But her cheeks had turned pink with excitement as she figured ten dollars would buy enough foodstuffs to make a profit two months in a row.

Matthew knew it and he smiled. "That's alright, ma'am. Maybe next time me and my boys come in, you can sport us a free dinner?"

Her face clouded up and she clutched his hand in hers. "Listen, Sheriff, I couldn't help but overhear what you boys were saying...and Mr. Hitchcock is correct. Sometimes it's just best to leave a rattlesnake in its hole." She cleared her throat and added, "I have been to too many funerals in the last couple of years and I think my old heart would break if I had to attend yours as well."

Matthew held the woman's hand for a moment. Then he tipped his hat, winked and said, "We'll be alright, ma'am. Just make sure you have some of that good pie left for when we return."

Henrietta watched as the handsome young sheriff walked out the door and tried not to shiver at the goose she felt walking over her grave.

The next morning was clear and cool when Matthew and his posse mounted up. They planned to head northeast into the Silver Valley area; Travis had heard that a couple of gang members were terrorizing a brothel just outside of one of the bigger mines.

Apparently, the miners—drunk and exhausted from their toils—were easy pickings as they took their meager paychecks to the whorehouse for some relaxation and relief. Even worse, it sounded like the madam of that establishment was being coerced into paying outrageous protection fees just to keep her girls from being beaten and robbed blind.

They were about ten miles out of town when Eggars said, "This ought to be a cakewalk, sir. Seems to me, all we need to do is hide in amongst the trees and nab those rascals as they come a ridin' up."

"Sounds good, Earl," Matthew said.

Then he gazed across a muddy field at a crowd of men standing, sitting, and walking slowly behind a high fence at the foot of a stony bluff. Covered in dirt and soot, they looked to be sagging with exhaustion. Other men sat on horses and stared down at them with sullen expressions, cracking long coiled whips in the air and barking orders.

Matthew saw something else. Well-dressed gentlemen in suits and ties—smoking cigars and chatting—stood far away from the mud inside of the fenced area. Matthew brought his horse to a stop and asked, "What is that over there? A prison?"

Travis and Hoss chuckled. "Nah, that's a mine,

Sheriff. Somebody found himself a nice hole and now he's got men working it for him and some Pinkertons to guard the cash."

Hoss leaned over sideways and spat in disgust. "May as well be a prison, I reckon. I swear, some of those poor fools get treated worse than any jailbird I ever heard of."

Matthew stared at the sorry sight for a moment and then shook his head. "Let's go!" he barked and spurred his horse into a trot, leaving the mine and the men working it far behind.

SOUTHERN COMFORT

MATTHEW AND HIS DEPUTIES STEPPED INSIDE THE brothel. It was neat and almost painfully clean. A Negro man was playing guitar in the far corner and four women sat in the parlor—two on a red brocade couch and two in matching gold armchairs—smiling enticingly at the newcomers.

The posse had arrived yesterday afternoon with the intention of grabbing any outlaw that had the misfortune to show his face. Unfortunately, no one matched the description on Matthew's warrants. In addition, the sheriff did not realize how close the brothel was to the mine's entrance gates...one hundred footsteps away at most and filled to bursting with pedestrians.

Matthew knew that an all-out snatch and grab would not work here so he and his team spent the night sleeping on the ground with their stars hidden away out of sight. Earlier that morning they had reconnoitered the little town, trying to gain information on the criminals' location without giving up the fact that they, themselves, were actually lawmen.

The stories were true, though; it sounded as if two or three members of the Mad Hatter gang showed up every other day or so to terrorize the whores, the miners, and even the local businessmen. Matthew also heard that the outlaws were picking unnecessary fights with the natives, mainly Crow and Nez Perce tribes who were already at war amongst themselves.

Retreating back to their makeshift camp, Matthew and the deputies decided to visit the whorehouse and ask some pointed questions like who exactly was doing the damage and what their names were. The sheriff had already decided to put the criminals in jail whether he held a warrant for their capture or not.

Matthew couldn't stand how the "Hatters" were not only robbing people of all their possessions but seemed to enjoy inflicting as much pain as possible while perpetrating their crimes. The owner of a small mercantile grew agitated as he recounted being robbed a month earlier.

"They just mosied in like they owned the place and started taking whatever they wanted off the shelves," he said. "Then, when I picked up my shotgun to chase 'em off, they shot me in the arm, came around the counter, grabbed my little girl Sarah, and held a knife to her throat! She is just a child!"

"Now," he continued, "I don't put up a fuss at all when they come in. I just ignore them while they rob me blind." Using his apron to sweat off his face, he glared. "What I want to know is where is the law around here, huh? My wife and I settled in this area because it seemed to be one of the more civilized places in this godforsaken country. But I haven't seen hide nor hair of any sheriff or marshal!"

Matthew stood still and fought the impulse to tell the man that his wish was coming true...that five lawmen were standing smack dab in front of him right now. Feeling his deputies growing restless behind him, he simply tipped his hat and said, "I am sorry for your troubles, sir. Tell me, do you happen to know what time that fancy house up the road opens for business? My boys and I have been on the trail for quite a while and would like to work the kinks out, if you know what I mean."

The man almost grinned. "Not until 6:00 pm, I hear. They are new to town and it seems like a pretty respectable place for what it is. Even the missus is impressed since they close down on Sundays and every one of them heads to the chapel to hear the word of God."

It was just after six in the evening now, and Matthew and the rest of the posse stood just inside the brothel's doorway. It was a good house, newly built with a small bar, a parlor and a stairway leading upstairs to the bedrooms. Matthew was just about to speak to one of the painted ladies when the Negro man stopped playing his instrument and walked over to them.

He was an attractive middle-aged man with dark

curls and luminous brown eyes. When he spoke, his southern drawl was as sweet as honey-wine. "Welcome to my establishment, gentlemen. My name is Antoine Robecheau." Looking at them in turn he smiled and added, "Five men...voila! I just happen to have five, beautiful ladies. One for each of you."

Matthew only counted four women and was about to say that he and his men were there for information rather than the man's wares when the most beautiful creature he had ever clapped eyes on walked slowly through an adjacent door. He heard Roy catch his breath and felt the other deputies stir behind him.

Matthew had never visited the southern states but he suddenly recalled his Uncle Jon's stories about some of the Creole courtesans—octaroons—he had seen and danced with when he was a younger man. He said they were the most exquisite females on the planet with pale but dusky skin, soft black hair and full breasts.

Well, he thought, *I must be looking at one right now.* Matthew stood up straight and tried not to let his desire show.

"Jumpin' Jehoshaphat!" Roy muttered and Matthew silently agreed.

The woman was dressed in a beautiful rose-colored chiffon gown. The neckline of her dress showed her silky, cafe au lait cleavage and her hair fell past her hips in wild abandon. Wide, brown eyes tilted up at the corners with mischievous mirth and, when she smiled, her teeth were as white and even as piano keys.

Those eyes appraised Matthew from the top of his

hat to the tip of his boots and then she crooked a long jewel-laden finger at him and beckoned. Matthew hesitated for a moment, then turned to his men. He tried not to let any of them catch his eye as he said, "I think it would be best to spend a little time here, don't you? For information and the like."

Three of the deputies were already fishing in their pockets for cash; apparently, they didn't mind staying and sampling the wares in the slightest. Music rose in the corner where Antoine was now playing the harmonica and the sound of southern blues filled the air as the prostitutes wound their arms around the men's bodies, smiling up at them in welcome.

Matthew didn't like to study himself and his own behavior too closely but he knew that something—a piece of his own heart—was hidden away from most people. He had not allowed himself to fall in love, ever. The closest he had come to letting loose of his tightly-held reservations was when he was with Iris Imes.

He was not, however, a virgin. He enjoyed a steady arrangement with a young woman in Spokane Falls named Madeline Barrows...a pretty thing with long, blonde hair and twinkly blue eyes. Although Madeline seemed to enjoy his company well enough, there were other men in town who could—and did—pay far better than Matthew Wilcox ever could so she never shed a tear when he left.

It had been months since his last visit, though, and he realized that his wits were not as sharp as they should be. His loins ached with longing and his nerves were stretched taut with tension as the beautiful Creole woman stepped up close to him, gazed into his eyes, and whispered, "My name is Chloe Robecheau. Come with me, cher."

As Matthew walked slowly up the stairs, he looked down and saw Travis and Roy sitting close to the brothel owner; Travis nodded at the young sheriff and winked as if to say, "*Good. You need the knots worked out of you...*"

He noticed the other deputies pairing off as well and then he was behind closed doors, losing himself in the jasmine-scented softness of Chloe's body.

As Matthew and the prostitute's bodies joined together in ecstasy, a different type of meeting was taking place fifty-five miles away. Top Hat was ready to make his move. He had assigned half his crew to worry the citizens of the Idaho Panhandle and a few other men south to the Oregon Trail vicinity.

"I want you men to do your best work while I'm gone on business. Steal what you can and get as much information as possible...and try not to get into it with the natives. I'm telling you, I have enough money to bail you out of trouble with the law but the Injuns ain't interested in cash," he lectured.

"And try not to kill anyone either, goddammit! Like I said, I can buy you out of most things but not the hangman's noose if a circuit judge grabs you."

He stared at each of his gang members and added, "The point of all of this is for you to create as much of a dust-up as possible while I circle around from behind and remove the man who threatens us all."

Taking off his dirty old hat, he scratched his jug-handled ears. "Normally, I would take out an enemy like that with one shot, but I've been doing some studying on the matter. Seems that the man's family is rich and his uncle, Jonathon Wilcox, is friendly with the Washington Territory governor and a few other fat cats out of D.C. I'm afraid if we approach this situation head on, we'll just get our own heads nipped clean off."

He put his hat back on and grinned. "So we're going in sneaky-like. Ike, Chollo, and me will take that pesky uncle out while you harry the sheriff and his posse here in Idaho territory. Pretty soon he will know the concept of steppin' out of the way of bigger men than him!"

The men burst into cheers at Top Hat's final words. He allowed them to puff up and celebrate for a moment, then he shouted, "Shut up! I got a few more words to say and then you can get on your way."

When the men stood before him in silence, he contin-ued, "Fair warning, fellas. This young sheriff is a fair shot from what I have heard. He is also good with a sword, for fuck's sake! I thought those things were out of style by now." He shook his head. "Still, a sword will kill you just as sure as a bullet, so step sharp. He's a game rooster, as are the deputies he's traveling with, so be careful. I don't want to leave and take care of business for this outfit just to come home to a bunch of dead men. Got it?"

Reminding them to rendezvous in Libby in three weeks, he watched as they gathered up their belongings and rode out of the encampment.

Three men remained with him: Ike Nelson, Chollo Gonzales, and Levon Smithers.

Top Hat had just finished smoking his cheroot when Ike murmured, "Do you really think they are good enough to stay ahead of Sheriff Wilcox and his deputies?"

"Nah, we'll lose half of 'em, at least. They are like a bunch of rodeo clowns, dressed up in funny clothes and waving ropes in the air but that's alright." Top Hat stared into the setting sun as the others digested his words.

Finally, Ike asked, "You starting up a new gang, Boss?"

"Yep," Top Hat murmured. "Got one lined up already…couple of men from my old outfit and a new boy who just made his way up from Tennessee. That one can shoot anything that moves from three hundred yards away with his Sharp's rifle."

He sat forward and spat a piece of tobacco leaf into the fire. Turning to face his trusted lieutenants, Top Hat added, "We'll drop that Jonathon Wilcox from such a distance he won't even know what hit him before he's standing in front of the pearly gates."

A FACT FINDING MISSION
GONE WRONG

LATER THAT EVENING, MATTHEW APPROACHED ANTOINE, Chloe's brother and business partner. Earlier, he had told the beautiful courtesan who he and his men were and stated their intentions, watching as she wept with newfound hope. Once Chloe told her brother the news, Antoine promptly locked the door for the night after pinning a note on it stating there was influenza in the house and that they were temporarily closed for business.

The siblings confirmed what Matthew had heard about the Mad Hatters' activities but, if anything, the whispered rumors didn't do justice to the real damage being perpetrated on the Robecheaus, their property, and the surrounding area.

Once a week or so, assorted members of Top Hat's gang swept into town robbing, pillaging and terror-izing the beleaguered citizens. Matthew already knew about the mercantile but he didn't realize just how bad things had gotten for everyone else. Rapes were common and many of the miners were now afraid to venture forth from their tents and hovels for fear of being set upon by outlaws.

The whorehouse, however, attracted the most attention. Seeing the newly constructed building and correctly assuming the Creoles possessed some wealth, the Mad Hatters focused most of their energy there. All of the girls had been repeatedly beaten and denied their agreed upon fees for services rendered; twice, Antoine and Chloe were held at gunpoint while the outlaws ransacked the house searching for hidden cash.

Unfortunately, the Robecheaus could not find their own muscle. Prostitution was not illegal, but brothel owners usually did not enjoy traditional police protection and were expected to employ their own security. The Pinkerton men were no use; they were too busy guarding the mine owner's precious metals to be distracted by the Robecheau's plight. The soldiers at the fort were preoccupied as well, rounding up Indians.

Most of the strong-arm men in town had already fled the area, unable and/or unwilling to be gunned down by the gang's overwhelming force. This left the Robecheaus alone and at the Hatters' mercy.

Antoine's eyes were shiny with frustration as he spoke to Matthew and his posse. "We don't ask for much," he whispered. "We come from Louisiana as free niggah's with a little money we saved from our younger days. Me as a music man and my little sister as an Octaroon fancy girl. We come all this way to run an honest business—a pleasure house for gentlemen—not to lose all our savings to outlaws."

Matthew replied, "We are sorry for your troubles, Mr. Robecheau, and we are trying to help. We have come to take these criminals to trial but we need a little help. Do you think you can keep our identities hidden for the next few days, just until the gang shows up again?"

Both Antoine and Chloe smiled. "I will tell my girls to stay quiet. They will be happy to do so if they know they will no longer be beaten and robbed," Chloe said.

Antoine added, "We have a room...it is small but perhaps you all can stay there hidden, oui?"

Turning to his deputies, Matthew saw them nod in agreement. Then Chloe stood and ordered her girls to move cots and pallets into an upstairs bedroom while Matthew asked his men to gather their belongings and bring them into the house, watching as they stepped outside to move camp.

The older man gestured and said, "Come wit me, Sheriff, please. I have something to show you."

He followed Antoine into the front parlor and watched as he picked up his fiddle. Turning around, he handed Matthew the musical instrument and said, "Look!"

Staring at the front and the back of the violin, he finally spied a tiny dowel close to the neck of the instrument. Glancing at Antoine, he silently asked permission and received a smile in return. Sitting down as Antoine closed and locked the back door leading into the parlor, Matthew took his pocketknife and gently inserted the tip into a grove by the dowel.

It took some doing as the piece was firmly anchored into the polished wood but he finally lifted the closure. The back of the fiddle came off in his hands and rolls of cash spilled into his lap and onto the floor. Matthew looked up into Antoine's gleaming brown eyes.

"You see?" he said softly. "Those bandits have not taken everything from me, no." His lips twisted as he added, "I always try to have my little fiddle in hand when the robbers come so, if the worst happens, my sister can start over with some money."

As the sound of hurried footsteps rushed past the parlor's closed door, he continued, "Since we are now the mouse who fights the cat...yes?" he grinned. "I wanted you to know where the cash is so Chloe will be taken care of if I am killed. Also..." He bent down and picked up one of the rolls of bills. "This is for you and your deputies."

Matthew shook his head but Antoine held one hand in the air. "I insist, Sheriff. We all need money, no? I would not have it said that Antoine does not reward his own angels."

There was a knock at the door and they heard Chloe call out, "Antoine...Sheriff, may I come in?"

"Just one moment, cherie," Antoine responded and then bent over, stuffed the fiddle with cash again and fastened the instrument closed. Placing it gently on a little wooden stand, he walked to the door and opened it.

"Come in, sister. The sheriff and I were just making plans for what is to come. Will you join us?"

Chloe stared at her brother's face, then at Matthew for a moment, before she sat in one of the matching armchairs.

"So what is this plan? she asked.

Two nights later, as six o' clock rolled around, Matthew and Roy sat at opposite ends of the small bar and waited for guests to arrive. It was past time for Top Hat's men to show up…almost a week had come and gone since their last visit. However, one of the girls—an older blonde from Kansas named Gloria—reported seeing three of the worst Hatters down at the mercantile earlier that day so the Robecheaus expected the outlaws to stroll in anytime.

One of the warrants had looked familiar to the girls and the brothel owners but they assured Matthew and his deputies that there were at least five criminals who showed up on a regular basis. They also assured Matthew they would make sure the lawmen knew who the criminals were.

Two times, Chloe answered a knock on the door and both times the sheriff knew that these were simply customers. One was an old man who immediately asked for a girl who looked young enough to be his granddaughter. Chloe confessed that the man—whose name was Denny Smith—usually asked for a foot massage and liked to talk about his children and grandchildren who were apparently back home in the Texas region.

The other customer, although quite young, looked and smelled like a cowboy or a shepherd. He stood in the front parlor, hat in hand, as Gloria got up, saying, "This one is mine, girls." Then she took him by the arm and said, "We need to get you washed up, son."

Matthew watched as she led the young man around the back door into a kitchen area where a tub was already set up and a kettle steamed with hot water. Soon, he heard the sound of splashing and a low, feminine chuckle.

A half-hour later, Matthew again heard pounding at the front door. Looking up, he saw Antoine and Chloe exchange glances and then turn to him, nodding; they had informed him that a harsh knocking usually heralded the gangsters' arrival.

The sheriff hunkered down in his chair, trying to appear inebriated. Roy did the same on the other side of the makeshift bar. The other deputies were hidden; Hoss and Earl upstairs in their room and Travis behind some large barrels in the pantry.

Chloe smoothed her blue, diaphanous skirt with shaking hands and took a deep breath. Then she walked to the front door and opened it wide. "Gentlemen, welcome back!" she exclaimed and stepped aside as three men crowded into the house.

Robecheau had grabbed his guitar from the wall and melancholy music filled the room. Roy pretended to be sleeping and Matthew tried to make his body loose, as though alcohol was the only thing keeping him upright. Peering through slitted lids into an elaborate, gilt-framed mirror in the corner, he saw one of his warrants standing behind him with two other men he didn't recognize.

Antoine suddenly switched tunes and a lively gig started up. Matthew jerked as if jolted awake and saw the brothel owner smile and wink at him, the prearranged signal that all the new guests were members of the Mad Hatter gang.

Sagging in his chair again, Matthew dropped his head so that his face was hidden by his hair. Staring through the golden strands, he saw the prostitutes display themselves like prize geese at a county fair. Then, one by one, the men walked upstairs with a woman on his arm.

As soon as the bedroom doors closed, Matthew stood up and walked into the pantry area. "Travis, you ready?" he whispered.

The older deputy stepped from the large closet and replied, "Yes, Boss, whenever you are."

The young cowboy sitting in the cooling water with the buxom blonde on his lap gaped at the sudden flurry of activity and the grim-faced men whom he had assumed were either drunk or asleep.

Looking down at the flustered man, Matthew asked, "Gloria, has this man had his fill?"

She grinned. "Yes, Sheriff, some time ago. He's as clean as a whistle by now, too."

Matthew kept a straight face and said, "Son, you

need to skedaddle out of here, right now. We are serving arrest warrants on some customers upstairs and I don't want to see an innocent bystander get hurt in the process."

The cowboy almost tossed Gloria out of the water as he hastened to make himself scarce. He was going to put his boots on outside but Matthew said, "No! You put 'em on right here...and, when you leave, I want you to act natural."

The young man sat down on a nearby chair and pulled on his boots with shaking fingers. Roy stuck his head around the doorjamb and nodded, letting him know the only other customer had finished his business and left.

Matthew escorted the cowboy out the front door. Turning around, he studied Antoine's face. The brothel owner winked and the sheriff locked the door again...he and his posse were alone with the outlaws. He gestured and three of the whores grabbed their pre-packed bags of valuables and hurried out the back.

"You should leave too, Antoine," Matthew whispered.

Antoine shook his head. "No. They are like scared rats, monsieur. They will come looking if the music stops. I stay right here and play my harp."

Matthew sighed as harmonica tunes filled the air and he glanced at the four deputies suddenly taking up space in the front parlor. Hoss and Earl had crept downstairs sometime in the last five minutes, joining Roy and Travis.

"Better get a move on," Hoss muttered. "I think a couple of those boys are finished already. They may be heading down here for a drink any minute."

Matthew nodded and whispered, "Let's go!"

The five men ran swiftly and silently up the stairs. One of the bedroom doors was already opening and Matthew saw a girl buttoning up her robe as she stepped into the hallway. Her eyes got big when she saw the sheriff and his deputies heading her way but she had the presence of mind to call out, "I'll be right back, honey, with some of that hooch!" Then she went running downstairs.

Hoss and Earl entered that bedroom with their guns drawn. At the same time, Matthew opened another door and saw one of the prostitutes using a wet rag to wash between her legs. There were tear tracks on her face, and he saw red bruise marks and scratches on the inside of her thighs. She turned away in shame.

Matthew's heart ached for her but he didn't have time to give comfort. In that split second of hesitation, the man on her bed had seen the threat and rolled off the far side next to the wall.

Matthew kept his .45 aimed at where the man's head disappeared but the outlaw shot at the sheriff's feet and legs from under the bed. He missed and, seconds later, Matthew reached him. "Put 'em up or I'll shoot you dead!"

There was a moment of relative silence and he heard Earl call out, "Sheriff? You all right?"

Matthew answered, "Yeah. How about you two?"

"We got our rooster, sir. All trussed up nice for the fire."

Matthew looked over at the bruised and beaten woman who now held her own gun on the scoundrel behind her bed. "You go on and get that other one, Sheriff. I got this skunk in my sights."

The fee would be higher if Matthew and his posse were able to bring the outlaws in alive but he was willing to take his chances. He knew that the next room down was Chloe's and he had just heard a muffled scream. He nodded at the whore and hollered, "Hoss, get in here and put this man in handcuffs!"

"Yes, sir!" came the reply.

Matthew ran the few steps down to Chloe's half-open doorway. Stepping inside, he suddenly understood why Roy and Travis were so quiet. Matthew knew that the chances of them being able to pull a snatch and grab in total silence were practically nil. Still, up until the outlaw opened fire on him, the sheriff had hoped and prayed he and his boys were going to pull it off.

As he stepped through Chloe's door, however, his hopes were dashed. Raymond Gallagher—the one man they held a warrant on—was lying on the rumpled sheets of the bed with Chloe's body stretched out on top of his. He held a small derringer to her temple and grinned at the three lawmen with crazy-eyed glee.

Both of the deputies held their pistols on the man but he seemed to have made himself small. There was not one square inch of him showing past the woman's body and no way to shoot without putting a hole in Chloe.

"Put down that gun! NOW!" Matthew barked.

For a moment, it seemed that Gallagher was going to give up. His arms sagged a little and he peered up past Chloe's long black hair to see who was addressing him. Matthew took aim and just about took a shot. But then he heard the man burst into laughter.

As Matthew and his two deputies stared in shock, Raymond Gallagher shot Chloe in the head and howled like a rabid dog. He tossed the Creole down on the floor, then jumped up and danced in place on the bed as Matthew, Roy and Travis filled him full of holes.

The dead outlaw fell and landed squarely on Chloe's body. In the ensuing silence, the only thing Matthew could hear was Antoine, who stood in the open doorway weeping with sorrow.

23

OLD ENEMIES

THE POSSE LEFT THREE DAYS LATER. BUT, FIRST, THERE was business to take care of. Matthew wired Sheriff O'Brian and asked him to send a wagon for the captured outlaws so they could stand trial and/or be laid to rest in Coeur d'Alene. The sheriff arrived the next day with two deputies and a mortician. He thanked Matthew for a job well done and told him that the younger of the two deputies was his for the duration of their hunt.

The gap-toothed man smiled and introduced himself. "It's my honor to help out, sir. My name is Kevin Short."

Although Matthew didn't really want more men, he acknowledged the fact that the Mad Hatters were a special brand of loco. He knew now that he needed as much manpower as possible and was finally beginning to understand his uncle's naked fear over the mission.

Welcoming Kevin on board, Matthew and the two

deputies rounded up the disgruntled prisoners and tossed them into the barred cage in the back of the wagon. Then they brought the wooden coffin containing Raymond Gallagher and fastened the box onto a special platform behind the cage.

As he left, O'Brian called out, "You take care now and come back home in one piece!" The words were aimed at the young deputy but Matthew realized the message was meant for him, too. Gritting his teeth, he watched as the wagon turned around in front of the whorehouse and headed back to O'Brian's hometown.

Antoine and his girls were busy inside the brothel. The night his sister died, Antoine decided to abandon his new brothel and take what remained of his stable to the greater Seattle area. Feeling responsible somehow for the Robecheau's calamity, Matthew ordered his deputies to help them pack up and move.

In the meantime, there was a Catholic burial to perform. The closest clergyman was in the Priest Lake area and he wasn't expected until later that night so Matthew took it upon himself to fix the bullet holes in the walls of the house. Most of the damage, of course, was in the two bedrooms upstairs.

He had repaired the lathe and painted one of the rooms yesterday but now he paused outside of Chloe's bedroom, suddenly overcome with fearful apprehension. Matthew had seen too much death in his life to let fear of dying get the better of him, but it had been a long time since someone close to him had passed on.

Taking a deep breath, he opened the door and

peered inside. Chloe was lying in state on the bed. Antoine and his girls had washed her body and combed her long, black hair so the bullet hole didn't show. She wore her finest gown but her beautiful face was ashy and her vibrant, golden eyes were weighted down with copper pennies.

Candles were burning and incense filled the air yet Matthew thought he could smell death's signature fragrance seeping like fog from that part of the room. Swallowing, he began to stuff the holes in the wall with old newspapers and took measurements for new lathing.

Working in silence, Matthew was acutely aware of the courtesan's corpse. As he toiled, he remembered the night he had lost himself in her fragrant warmth. She had taken a hold of him and run her tongue up and down his belly and over his nipples until he panted with desire. When he tried to bring her body down upon him, though, she had giggled and taken the whole of him into her mouth.

Matthew stopped working and stood in the darkened room, shuddering. Then he heard a voice and turned to see Antoine standing in the doorway.

"My God, Sheriff! There is no need for you to work in here," he said softly. "The man who bought this house from me knows very well what happened. That is why he got it for such a cheap price." Seeing how anxious the young man was, he stepped close and clasped Matthew's arm. "Come, cher. I hear the priest is in town now. We should go down and welcome him in."

Matthew followed Antoine out and felt another chapter of his life close as the doorknob clicked into place.

The next morning, Matthew, his posse, Antoine, his girls, and a number of the community's citizens attended Chloe Robecheau's funeral. It was a beautiful day; fluffy white clouds sailed across azure skies and the sun's warmth was finally taking its toll on the area's incessant mud. The priest droned on in Latin and many of the attendees were starting to wipe sweat from their brow.

Matthew prayed for a quick end to the service. He was restless now and, despite feelings of lingering guilt over what had happened to the beautiful Octaroon, old familiar feelings of rage, revenge and retribution had swamped his soul sometime the night before as he tossed in his bed.

He had woken up repeatedly, images of naked women filling his mind. The slightly menacing but erotic dreams turned into nightmares when Chloe's dark body suddenly became pale with peach-colored freckles, abundant breasts and masses of long, red hair. Matthew had gazed up into Iris's face as she sat astride him but he saw nothing but blood.

Sitting up in bed with a cry, he met Travis' eyes. The old man was sitting by the windowsill smoking a cheroot and he whispered, "Settle down, son. We all need to get some sleep for the task ahead."

Sighing, the deputy tossed the cigar out the window, closed it, and lay down on his pallet with his face turned to the wall. Matthew sat awake for a while and then closed his eyes, willing himself back to sleep.

Four hours after the funeral service ended, Matthew and his posse said their goodbyes to Antoine Robecheau and his girls and rode north. Their next stop was somewhere between Sandpoint and Bonner's Ferry. Apparently, a whole village had been burned to the ground when some of the citizens took up arms in defense of their local saloon and telegraph office. Most of the town was in ruins but a few people remained, determined to start over again and hopeful that a sheriff's posse may be able to remove the outlaws from the region.

They rode at a crisp pace but Matthew allowed himself to take in the scenery even as he watched for hidden threats. Tall, tree-covered hills rose up into majestic mountains. Some of the peaks were so high, snow still painted their pinnacles white while the valleys below bloomed with wildflowers and green grass as high as the horses' bellies.

There was a stand of aspen and birch trees to their right, their tiny leaves shimmering in the sunlight. As Matthew gazed at them, he heard Hoss shout, "Lookit, Boss! That would fill our bags for the trip ahead."

Matthew turned and saw two young bucks running across the meadow, moving swiftly as if they had been spooked from their afternoon grazing.

They were about fifty miles—or two days away

from Sandpoint—so what Hoss said was correct. Stocked up with hardtack, coffee, biscuits and beans, they were seriously short on meat. The smaller of those two bucks would see him and his deputies through the next couple of days and what they didn't finish could be shared amongst the citizens they were trying to protect.

Hoss and Earl looked at him with ill-concealed excitement but when he nodded in approval and said, "Just one, alright?" they grinned and broke out their rifles. Cocking the weapons, both men spurred their horses and took off after the deer.

Matthew, Travis, Roy and the new man Kevin sat their horses and watched as Hoss and Earl rode up fast on the bucks. Then Hoss reined his horse sideways, lifted his rifle and shot at the smaller of the two animals.

Matthew and his men shouted with glee as the animal stumbled and fell down in the long grass. They kicked their horses into a run in order to help Hoss with his prize but pulled up short as something strange happened. They were too far away to see clearly but Matthew heard Earl shout in panic, then saw Hoss grab his own neck in shock.

"Holy shit! Indians are attacking 'em!" Travis muttered.

Matthew saw it now. About ten braves were hidden in amongst the trees that bordered the meadowland. All of them were mounting their ponies and racing toward Hoss and Earl even as he and his deputies approached from the opposite direction. He could hear their whooping cries and wondered whether they were from the Coeur d' Alene or Spokane tribes.

"Goddammit!" he snarled as Hoss fell to his knees in the grass. Matthew was close enough now to see the arrow sticking out from his deputy's neck and watch the blood running in sheets down his stout chest.

"They are not going to take those men's scalps!" he yelled. "Get ready to fight, boys!"

Letting out a cry of his own, Matthew spurred his horse, pulled his pistol out of its holster, and raced to meet the Indians head on.

24

REDBIRD

GUNS ROARING, MATTHEW AND HIS DEPUTIES RODE FAST into the small band of Indians. As he drew closer, the sheriff realized this was most likely a Nez Perce hunting party as some of their ponies were dragging wooden travois' with dead animal carcasses piled high on them.

He also noticed that most of the Indians were young boys and teenagers probably tasked with finding meat while the older braves made war against the white men who were trying to take their land or with other tribes that aligned themselves on the side of their enemies. Although the Nez Perce were a peaceful people who strived to get along with their white neighbors, there were factions within the tribe who refused to give up and move onto reservations.

Matthew's heart ached; he didn't like killing kids, Indian or otherwise. But as he watched, one of the boys slid off his horse and knelt in the tall grass—knife in hand—to take Hoss's scalp.

"No!" he cried.

The youngster gazed up at him for a moment and then proceeded to saw at Hoss's hair. Matthew lifted his pistol, aimed and pulled the trigger. The boy screamed as his body flew backward on the grass; he clutched his right arm, weeping with pain, as Matthew turned away to deal with another older boy riding hard in his direction.

The teenager on horseback howled and held his tomahawk high in the air. Just as the Indian let his weapon fly, Matthew ducked, lifted his right boot and watched as his heel slammed against the pony's long nose. The animal reared up, kicking in panic, and the boy yelled "Iieeeee!" as he fell and landed hard on his back in the grass.

The sheriff realized his deputies had come to the same conclusion...they were being attacked by children! Alone and unprotected, the last thing a sensible posse wanted to do was provoke the wrath of a hostile tribe of Indians like the mighty Nez Perce.

Matthew spurred his horse and shouted, "Aim high, men! Don't shoot to kill!"

It was hard to hear over the boys' war cries but the sheriff saw his men nod in understanding and thought he heard Travis shout, "Hear you, Boss!"

By now, five of the young men lie prostrate on the grass. None of them seemed badly hurt but, before the posse had a chance to subdue them all, Matthew saw the remaining teenagers kick their ponies into a gallop and take off fast toward the tree line. Looking down, he searched for Hoss and saw him lying about twenty-five feet away.

The deputies stood their horses and gazed down at Hoss as well. Earl spat and groaned, "Goddammit! What am I gonna tell Martha?"

"You tell her that he died in the line of duty," Matthew replied, stepping down off his horse with a sigh. Turning to the other deputies, he added, "Men, we need to secure these cubs and render what medical aid they might need, okay? We do not want to get caught up in a damn war!"

Travis, Roy and Kevin approached the prone youngsters with ropes and guns in hand. A few of them —more angry than hurt—struggled to get away and cried out in fear but the deputies trussed them up in a wink, forcing the weeping and humiliated teens into helpless captivity.

One of them, however, was gunshot. Matthew examined him and nodded in satisfaction; the bullet had grazed the boy's upper arm and, although it bled profusely, he would survive to fight another day. The sheriff grabbed his medicinal kit, pressing some clean cloth pads against the wound. The young brave stared up at him with scared eyes and murmured something Matthew didn't understand.

Travis knelt at the boy's side and murmured, "Steady, son...this is gonna smart." While Matthew stood up and got out of the way, Travis wrapped long pieces of cloth around the youngster's arm to keep the pads in place.

The teen's eyes rolled back in their sockets but, when Matthew placed his finger on the boy's throat, the pulse was strong and steady. The other boy who had flown off his pony was bound up tight on the ground. When he saw Matthew and Travis tend to the smaller boy, he shouted something in fear and defiance. Looking between the two teenagers, Matthew realized they must be brothers as the resemblance was uncanny.

There was something else about the two that made Matthew frown in consternation...they looked familiar to him for some reason. Shrugging off the temporary déjà vu, the sheriff and his deputy moved away as the older boy scooted toward his brother and peered down into his face. Seeing that his sibling still breathed, he glared at the lawmen and then sat staring at the ground under his crossed legs.

Finally, the prisoners tended to and secured, Matthew and the rest of the posse walked over and looked at Hoss. There was a long gash at his hairline but very little blood and Matthew figured the arrow that had pierced the deputy's throat from front to back must have killed him quickly.

Sighing, Matthew said, "We need to get him wrapped up so we can take him on in to Sandpoint. Right, Earl?"

Earl stood staring down at his friend with his hat in his hands. "That would be proper, Sheriff. I think his people might want to fetch him back home if we move fast enough."

Travis said, "If I recall correctly, there's a good doc in Sandpoint. He'll get Hoss fixed up and ready for a proper plantin'."

"Damn stupid kids," Roy muttered in disgust while eying the encroaching trees. "Why did they have to go and choose our party to count coup?"

Matthew felt the same ominous chill and he replied, "I know, Roy. But at least none of them got killed and that's what counts. Still, we best move quickly."

Kevin fetched a large canvas tarp from one of the pack mules and spread it out on the ground close to Hoss's body. Carefully, and with as much respect as possible, they rolled the big man's corpse over and over so the tarp covered him head to toe. Grunting with the effort, they hefted Hoss over his now saddleless horse and tied him securely in place.

Matthew took a final moment to check the Indian prisoners. Fetching a canteen of water, he also left a sack of biscuits for them to share. He sincerely doubted, though, they would starve or die from thirst before their tribe members sent out a search party.

"We better skedaddle, Boss," Travis said as Matthew walked up to his horse and rummaged in his bags.

"Just give me a minute, Travis. I don't want to take any chances," Matthew said.

Fishing around in his saddlebags, he found a faded blue handkerchief. Fashioning it to the end of a long branch like a flag, he stuck it upright in the ground.

He mounted his horse and, staring down at the boys, he said, "I don't know if any of you speak English but, just in case, be careful the next time you try to count coup on a band of armed deputies. I'm sure your people are already on their way to find you, but you tell your father and uncles that we didn't start this...you did!"

Five sets of dark eyes followed the white men as they trotted off into the setting sun.

A few hours later, Redbird and a number of his warriors followed three young boys back to the meadowlands. The days were long although it was late enough now that shadows fell in pools across much of the valley. Still, there was enough light to see a small blue cloth hanging listlessly from a tall stick about a hundred yards past the trees.

The boys were anxious to rescue their hunting companions but stopped their ponies and sat silently when their war chief barked an order for them to stay still and shut up. Redbird was furious with the lot of them and afraid of what he might find under that little flag.

The youngsters had told him the white men were fiends from hell, with weapons spitting sound and fire all at once. They confessed that they were outgunned and did not realize that the men were soldiers of some sort until it was too late. Every boy there also knew that just as soon as the rescue party got back to the village, they would be severely punished.

"You stay here," Redbird told the boys as he and

four of his warriors walked their horses past the tree line into the pasture. They approached slowly and could hear the sounds of voices coming from up ahead. Sighing with relief, Redbird also heard his older boy Matthew telling the others to be quiet.

Suddenly furious again, Redbird decided to teach his sons and their friends a lesson. Catching the eye of one of his warriors, he winked and then let out a blood-curdling screech. His fighting braves did the same and spurred their ponies into a fast gallop.

They circled the boys on the ground, yelling insults and taunts in the dark, and he heard his older son call out, "Father, is that you?"

Losing the heat of his anger, Redbird brought his mount to a halt. Sliding off his pony, he approached the youngsters who were tied up together on the ground where a canteen and the remnants of some meal were spread out between them. He also saw his youngest son sitting up though obviously in great pain with a bloody bandage tied around his right arm.

"We are sorry…" Matthew started to say but closed his mouth quickly when he saw the look in his father's eyes.

Redbird knelt by Jacque's side and studied the field dressing on his son's arm. Whoever had done this did a good job, Redbird decided with relief. The boy stared up into his face and whispered. "Are you going to punish us, Father?"

He sighed but said, "I think you have had enough

punishment. But your brother and his friends...yes, they will be punished as soon as we get home."

Matthew stared at the ground beneath his toes and wished he could just disappear like smoke from a fire. His father did not use capital force very often but, when he did, the experience was painfully memorable.

Strangely, the men who his sons had attacked left them their horses and a warrior walked up with one now while the other braves cut the ropes off the remaining boys' arms and legs. They scrambled to mount their ponies and waited until Redbird mounted his own.

"I will carry my son...hand him to me," he said and young Jacques was placed gently into his father's arms.

Within moments of the Indian's disappearance into the forest, a female cougar and her two kittens were tearing silently at a dead deer that lay forgotten in the tall grass.

ONWARD CHRISTIAN SOLDIERS

THE NEXT TWO DAYS WERE SAD AND FRUSTRATING FOR Sheriff Wilcox and his deputies. They traveled the remaining forty-eight miles into Sandpoint without incident but, twice, Hoss's body had slipped down off the horse's back. He had been overweight with most of his bulk in his upper body so, no matter how many clever ways they thought of to secure him, he kept tipping over to one side or the other.

In addition, summer had finally made an appearance. It was in the high 90s by the time they reached town and Hoss's corpse was beginning to stink. This upset Earl to no end ánd the animals, too; they shied and snorted, both at the burden they carried and at the darting shadows of carrion birds circling in the hot, flawless sky.

When they got to within ten miles of town, Matthew sent Earl ahead to secure a wagon and a few bales of ice, if there was any to be found. After the deputy rode away, Matthew led Hoss's horse to a small stream. Roy and Travis followed on foot while Kevin Short took care of their mounts, hobbling them off the side of the wagon trail in some tall grass.

The three men untied the ropes around Hoss's body and wrestled the corpse onto the ground. A loud, farting noise came from within the tarp and Roy jumped back in alarm.

"Holy shit! Is he still alive?" he asked with a tremor of fear in his throat.

"No, Roy...you know better. It's just body gasses escaping, I suspect," Matthew said even as he suppressed his own shudder of revulsion.

Travis added, "Well, natural or not, I will be happy to get this man buried and be on our way." He walked off, leading Hoss's horse over to where the others grazed.

Matthew and Roy stared down at the tarp-covered body and said their farewells. Then they joined the others and waited for the wagon to arrive, which it did about three hours later. They saw a small plume of dust on the horizon and a couple of riders accompanying it. Fifteen minutes later Earl, Sandpoint's sheriff and another man rode up.

"Winston is the name," an old man with white whiskers said, "and this here is the town doctor, Samuel Thompson. Hear you got a dead deputy?"

"Yes, sir, we do. He's over there waiting for your arrival," Matthew answered. His tone was sharper than he intended yet he couldn't help but take offense at the sheriff's flippant tone of voice.

The old man looked startled and then swept his hat off his head as the doctor got down off his horse and told Earl to move the wagon closer to the dead body.

"I'm sorry, son," Winston said. "I have been at this job too long, I guess...makes a man cold. I didn't mean any disrespect to you or yours, though."

Matthew stood in the hot sun and felt a trickle of sweat run down his back. He was tired and heartsick, frustrated and uneasy. The last day and a half, as he and his remaining deputies traveled to this little town, Matthew had felt as if eyes were watching his back...an amused, malevolent gaze that measured his every decision and found them laughably ill-conceived.

He thought, at first, that the Indian boy's tribe was coming after them with revenge in their hearts but dismissed that idea after he and his posse traveled over thirty miles without any sign of attack. *No*, he thought, *this is something else. A premonition of some kind or a warning of impending doom.*

Staring at the old sheriff, Matthew mustered his manners and held out his hand to shake. "It's me who should be apologizing. It has been a rough trip overall, and a sad one as well. Thank you for bringing a cart out for my deputy. I would like him to have some dignity now that his time has come...at least more than my boys and I have been able to offer."

Winston nodded and said, "Looks like the men have

got it, Sheriff." Matthew turned to look and saw the wagon with Hoss's body in back heading their way.

The doctor hollered to them, "If it's okay with you, I would like to take this man on into town while there's still some daylight left."

Winston shouted, "Go on ahead, Sam. We'll be along shortly."

Turning back to Matthew, he added, "I told the missus that you boys were coming and she has set to making a fine dinner. Why don't we get going? You boys can get washed up, eat some good food and sleep in beds tonight instead of on the ground."

Matthew smiled with genuine gratitude, as did his fellow deputies. In their mad race away from the young Indians, they had forgotten all about the dead deer and were forced to choke down cold biscuits and jerky. They also stank with the sweat of leftover fear and hot temperatures. Mounting their horses, Matthew and his posse followed the grizzled, old sheriff into Sandpoint, Idaho.

Mrs. Winston had outdone herself. After Matthew and his deputies visited the town's bathhouse and donned fresh clothes, they ambled over to the sheriff's modest home and sat down to a dinner of fried chicken, mashed potatoes, gravy and string beans. There were fresh biscuits as well and sweet, raspberry jam.

Stout black coffee and peach pie was served after dinner and the lawmen sat at the table, trading stories about the outlaws who had made their lives and their duty such a burden in recent years.

After recounting many of the gang's evil deeds in his area, Winston said, "Good news is, I think our bad apples have up and left!" He took a sip of his coffee and continued, "Honestly, I wouldn't dream of turning away a helping hand and you boys showing up to chase those devils off is the best thing that has happened to this town in a long time."

He lit a stogie and stared at Matthew through the smoke. "My deputies and I try to keep an eye on the gang's movements, you know. Well, about two weeks ago, the bunch that keeps us company packed up and moved east like they were heading into Montana territory. Good riddance to bad rubbish, I say, but it looks to me like your services are no longer required."

"How about Bonner's Ferry?" Matthew inquired. "Have you heard news from those folks?"

Winston nodded, "Yup. Same story there, Sheriff. It's as though the whole gang has decided to pull up stakes and get the hell out of here...maybe they heard you and your boys were headed this way."

"I doubt if that worried them over much," Matthew responded. That same feeling—that itch of apprehension —was tickling the back of his neck again and Matthew shifted in his chair. He suddenly ached for some fresh air and a good night's sleep; he was not immune to fear but he was unaccustomed to these kinds of nervous vapors.

Sitting up straight, Matthew smiled and said, "Sheriff, I want to thank you for the fine meal and your welcome words but I think my boys and I could use some rest. We have been sleeping with one eye open the last three days in a row."

"Yes, sir." Winston smiled. "Like I said, the missus has made up the beds upstairs. There is plenty of room since my two daughters flew the coop. And there are privy pots and a little widow's walk if you want to smoke. Sound good?"

"Sounds great, Sheriff," Matthew answered and heard his deputies echo his words of thanks.

Earl had ridden home earlier to deliver the news of Hoss's demise to his widow, Martha, which left four men to share two beds. Although he would rather have had the fine double-bed to himself, he offered to share his mattress with Roy and heard the other two deputies in the next room do the same. Despite Roy's loud snores, Matthew closed his eyes and fell into a deep, dreamless sleep.

The next morning dawned bright and clear; it was going to be another hot day. Breakfast was laid out on a sideboard: scrambled eggs, bacon, tomatoes, and biscuits along with a note that read, *Come down to the office. See you soon. Sheriff Winston.*

The four men ate, taking care to wash and rinse their dishes when they were done as Mrs. Winston was nowhere to be seen. Then they grabbed their things and walked down Main Street toward the sheriff's office.

As soon as they stepped onto the porch, they saw

Winston jump up from his chair and gesture to someone outside the window. Standing still, they heard singing coming from across the street.

Mrs. Winston and some other women burst into song apparently aimed at them. *Onward Christian Soldiers,* they sang, as passersby stared. A few whores, taking the sun up the road, snorted with laughter at the expressions on the faces of Matthew and his deputies.

Matthew felt mortified and wished the women would stop but he doffed his hat and tried to smile as graciously as possible. He understood that the only thing standing between death and the good life for many of the citizens in the Northwest Territories was the long arm of the law.

People like him and his deputies represented order and safety and, although it sounded as if their services were not needed, the womenfolk were profoundly grateful that they had showed up to render assistance.

The song finally ended and—after elbowing Roy— Matthew and his posse bowed slightly and smiled their thanks. Then they ducked quickly inside the sheriff's office, slamming the door shut.

Sheriff Winston grinned at them and said, "Sorry about that, boys. I tried to talk the missus out of it but she insisted. Besides, she has a few new members in her choir. I suspect she's been itchin' to see how they were going to do."

Matthew thought his cheeks must still be red with embarrassment but he said, "That's okay, Sheriff. My boys and I have been in tighter spots than that before."

To which Travis replied under his breath, "But they wasn't half as humiliating."

"Oh! This came in this morning." Winston lifted a sheet of paper and handed it to Matthew. "Looks like you best move fast back home."

Matthew stared down at the telegraph in his hand: OUTLAWS HERE NOW stop> COULD USE ASSISTANCE stop> BEST HASTE stop> SHERIFF O'BRIAN, CDA stop>

Returning the missive to Roy, Matthew extended his hand to shake and said, "Guess we best be on our way, Sheriff. My boys and I thank you again for your hospitality."

The older man smiled and said, "You tell Sheriff O'Brian to wire me if he needs more men, alright?"

Matthew nodded and said, "Will do. Say, is the mercantile open this early? We could use a few victuals and some oats for the trip back."

"Sure," Winston replied. "And you tell that old crook, Aubrey, to put your supplies on my tab."

Matthew and his deputies made their farewells and then walked down the road to the local mercantile. A scrawny, sour-faced man sat at the counter and stared suspiciously at every item they placed in front of him. But he brightened when Matthew told him to charge their purchases to the sheriff's department.

Twice, Matthew caught the eye of an old Indian man who stood behind some barrels at the back of the store. He seemed to be shopping for pots, pans and the like but he smiled politely at Matthew's friendly expression. Twenty minutes later, he slipped out the door just as Matthew and his posse members were loading their purchases onto their horses, preparing to hit the road again.

He smiled in relief. Redbird's uncle, Swallow Feather, was still useful and, for that, he was proud. Although his old bones ached and he had lost the vision in his right eye, he had sharp hearing and even spoke some words of the white man's language.

As he stood in the mercantile, he had heard the sheriff's posse members say they were heading back the way they came…from Coeur d' Alene. That would most likely mean they would pass right by the place his foolish great-nephews had chosen to attack.

Although he did not know what his nephew, Redbird, wanted to do to the sheriff and his deputies, Swallow Feather was sure that it was something the white lawmen would never forget…if they lived to remember it at all.

THE ENEMY OF MY ENEMY

MATTHEW AND HIS MEN MADE HASTE BACK DOWN THE wagon trail from which they came. They were able to travel much more quickly now that they were not carrying a dead man and, by afternoon of their second day out, they came to the valley in which they had earlier engaged the Indian boys.

Matthew stopped their progress and, getting off his horse, he pulled his uncle's powerful telescope out of his saddlebag and glassed the wide valley as thoroughly as possible. The sun cast shimmering heat waves into the air and some sort of pollen lifted up from the meadow grass and wildflowers like yellow smoke.

"See anything?" Roy asked.

"No. I think that tribe must be long gone by now," Matthew murmured.

"Well, I would like to get past this valley and into a more populated area before nightfall," Travis said. "If'n you didn't mind traveling in the dark, Sheriff, we could be in Coeur d'Alene by ten o'clock or so."

Remembering the chill premonition that had run its cold tongue up and down his back the last few days, Matthew nodded in agreement. "I like that plan, Travis. It's about four miles through this valley. Let's move quickly and keep our eyes peeled as we go."

Mounting their horses, the men heeled the animals into a trot. As before, the aspens and birch trees dazzled the eye and it felt as if the stony toes of the Bitterroot Mountains flexed toward them in the lazy summer haze.

They had traveled about two miles when the posse's worst fears came true; they spotted the first wave of braves approaching them from an angle on their left at about the same exact location the earlier altercation had taken place.

Matthew and his deputies grabbed their weapons. No one spoke a word but they all knew that they were massively outnumbered and outgunned. It was rare to see such a well-armed band of fighting braves and Matthew wondered uneasily if the young boy he shot had somehow succumbed to what he thought was a minor flesh wound.

"Damn…" he whispered with regret. "I'm sorry, boys, but I think we're done for."

Suddenly, Roy said, "Jesus, would you look at that!"

Matthew and his deputies turned around in their saddles and stared as another wave of braves approached from behind on their right. There were at least thirty more Indians in this new group and, as they watched, the warriors melded together as one, forming into a great moving circle around them.

Strangely, they were silent. Watchful, yes, and armed to the teeth. But, in Matthew's experience, when Indians were about to engage in battle they were vocal about it, using their war cries as a terror-tactic as much as their spears, clubs and arrows.

"Put your weapons away, men…very slow and careful," Matthew said. "I think these boys are here to parlay."

He could only hope he was right. The one thing he and his posse *did* have was firepower but he sensed that something else was at play here, something that depended deeply and fiercely on mutual respect and trust.

As soon as Matthew and his men stowed their weapons, the circling Indians brought their ponies to a standstill, all of them facing the posse. They were festooned with war paint but their expressions were both peaceful and cautious, as though they knew very well they were interfering with powerful white men yet simply had no other choice.

As Matthew watched, a small hole opened within the circle and three more Indians approached slowly. To his amazement, he recognized two of the ponies and their riders; one was the boy he had shot and he assumed the other was his older brother. Another

Indian towered over the young braves and, although he was too far away to see clearly, it was plain that it was the tribe's chief who approached.

An attractive fellow with long braids and a high topknot decorated with beads and feathers, he wore an elaborate chest plate and a long, fur-lined cloak. Breathing easier, Matthew knew then that his instincts were correct; this was a peace talk—or parlay—not an attack.

"Get down off your horses, men. I think that chief wants to talk," he said softly.

"Well", Travis answered, "I sure hope he knows English or it's going to be a short chat."

They slid off their horses and stood looking at the slowly approaching riders. Five Indian braves broke rank, following the chief and the two boys as they came to a halt in front of the sheriff and his men.

Matthew stared up at the chief's face and squinted against the blazing sun. There was something familiar about the man and, suddenly, his eyes grew wide with alarm. *It's Redbird!* He thought in a panic, almost reaching for his revolver.

He had lost track of the nightmares that came to visit him over the years since his first encounter with Redbird during the terrifying journey with Randall Penny's band. Yet he understood that Top Hat had done something horrible to Redbird's brother and the Indian had sought justice, as he himself was doing now. Still, Matthew remembered that fateful day in the driving snow when first Parker and then Tulu had died while he bled in terror.

Swallowing the fear that threatened to overwhelm his good sense, he watched as the war chief climbed down from his pony, took two steps in his direction, and said, "Matthew. We need to talk."

Redbird had a secret. Something he admitted to no one, not even his beloved wife, Moon on Water...formerly known as Marie Dupre'. Ever since he had seen a small boy take out his weapon and, with one shot, put the big Negro out of his misery, Redbird had held a secret fascination with that boy's progress through life.

Of course, part of this was because Moon had spoken about the boy-child she called Mattie many, many times over the years. The great war chief might even have grown jealous over his wife's memories but for the fact that she was good and beautiful beyond measure, and the mother of his two sons.

Redbird understood that childhood friendships were very strong. He also knew there was a deep well of power within this particular young man; a potent medicine he had admired that day long ago and grew to appreciate more and more as the years flew by.

He had sent out scouts over the years to bring news of Matthew's recovery and his development as a white warrior. He knew about the wolf that had aligned itself with him...a wolf totem, just as his was. Redbird had heard about the young man's appointment as sheriff almost before Matthew did and that he had assembled a posse to search for their shared enemy, Top Hat.

Redbird also knew that Sheriff Wilcox had freed the small band of Nez Perce Indians who were trying to make their way to the tribe's larger village and that Matthew's namesake had tried to count coup on his mother's childhood friend...a deed that earned his eldest son a whipping from both his parents.

Now, as the mighty war chief studied the young sheriff, he realized he had been right about Matthew Wilcox. Those green eyes he remembered studied the world in cool appraisal and stunning intelligence. Redbird saw the sheriff's reaction to threat—an almost instinctual move to grab the big gun resting on his right hip—and saw how the man paused as if weighing the odds of his men's survival against his own fear. *If only half of my braves were as smart as this man...*

"Redbird." Matthew struggled to keep his voice from shaking, even as his deputies stirred behind him and many of the braves who sat their ponies bent toward each other, whispering in astonishment. "What can my men and I do for you today?"

The older Indian smiled. "Young Slingshot, how is your wolf?"

Matthew wondered how Redbird knew about Bandit but now was not the time to ask questions or demand answers.

"He is fine, sir," he said.

Redbird nodded and then spoke, "First, my sons owe you and your men an apology." Turning around he spoke in his native tongue and the two boys slid off their ponies and approached.

The younger boy, his arm in a leather sling, smiled bashfully but the older boy was as defiant as ever. He did, however, hand Matthew a piece of cloth and said, "Sorry…," before he pulled his little brother behind their father.

Matthew gazed at Redbird then opened the pale-colored cloth and saw a childish scrawl: *Mattie, plez exuse moi boys and husband. I am so happy. Go wit God. Marie.*

Finally, it felt like the weight of the world had been lifted off his shoulders. Marie was alive with sons of her own and happy with the war chief. He wasn't sure how he felt about that part of it but, nevertheless, his lungs heaved with relief.

Redbird watched the young sheriff's face and knew he had done the right thing. His people and Matthew's people might be at war and forever at cross purposes. His own *weyekin* had said as much, many times.

But there was a time in every man's life when a perceived enemy must become a friend in order to appease the spirit world. For Redbird, that time was now. He had one gift to give the young man before he and the rest of his tribe traveled overland to Bear Paw Mountain…the gift of information.

Glancing behind him, he signaled to his son and his warriors that it was almost time to go. Turning to Matthew, he said, "Slingshot, I have news I thought you should hear. The outlaw you and I both know—the man with the big hat—he is going to your home, your family."

He stared into Matthew's shocked eyes and added, "Go now, young wolf, before it is too late!"

Then Redbird and his sons were gone. The Indians circled their ponies again, voices raised high in a sound both plaintive and wild as Matthew and his posse watched them disappear into the trees.

A PERILOUS ROAD

MATTHEW STOOD STILL AS THE INDIANS RODE AWAY, HIS deputies unwilling to intrude upon the young man's thoughts as none of them knew how he had come to be on speaking terms with the Nez Perce war chief or what they could expect from their boss at Redbird's news.

After a moment, Matthew said, "I have to leave you now. Redbird is many things but I don't believe he is a liar. Roy, I expect you will follow me back home?"

Roy answered, "Of course."

Matthew nodded and turned to the other deputies. "You two should make haste for home. I think your troubles are my fault—at least, in part—and this whole chase was a diversion engineered by Top Hat to divide and separate the law around here... to make us weaker." He sighed. "If I could, I would go back with you and put those dogs down for good. But I need to go home and save my own people."

Travis was already mounting his horse. "Son, accompany us another five miles or so. I know of a route that cuts through the mountains and will put you in the flatlands about thirty miles from Spokane Falls."

Matthew tried to smile his thanks but his face was frozen with fear. Climbing up on own his horse, he said, "Let's head out."

An hour later, Travis pulled up and the party stopped alongside as he pointed into the forest to his right. "See that trail, yonder? It ain't much more 'n a game trail but it cuts through a crotch in these high hills pretty easy. I haven't been up this way for a few years but the trees have been cleared away and there is an old cabin about the halfway mark where you can rest up."

Matthew was ready to rowel his horse but he stopped long enough to thank Travis and Kevin for their help. "I hope you two will haul the mule back for me. I'll send someone later to fetch him but, right now, we only need our horses and two spares."

Travis nodded. Staring into Matthew's face, he could not help but wonder if he would be attending the young man's funeral long before someone came to fetch a wayward mule. Still, he wished Matthew and Roy well, adding, "Just as soon as we get those crooks sorted out, I will come to your aid and bring as many able-bodied men as I can muster. I will also ask Sheriff O'Brian to wire the deputies in Spokane Falls."

The deputies then spurred their horses toward home as Matthew and Roy picked their way up a thin path of cleared rock and grass heading into the forested foothills. Night was falling rapidly and made gloomier by the tree cover. Yet a sliver of moonlight illuminated the trail enough that they traveled another sixteen miles before coming across a small hut.

Matthew's heart yearned to press on but they had been riding more than twenty hours and the horses were blown and footsore. He also knew that, if he and Roy didn't get some rest, they would be useless in the upcoming conflict.

Moving silently in the clearing, the two men walked up to the cabin door with their guns drawn. Knocking at the wooden shingle, they listened intently for signs of life but heard only the startled hoot of an owl in the dusky shadows.

Matthew pushed the door open and saw that the place was indeed empty. Although he had cursed the summer heat a number of times over the last few days, he was thankful now; he did not want to start a fire and take a chance of alerting the bandits—or anyone else, for that matter—to their presence.

They ate cold chuck, drank tepid water from their canteens, and spoke little before lying down on their saddle blankets to sleep. Roy wondered how much of a jump the outlaw known as Top Hat had on them and how Jon Wilcox was holding up. The two deputies he had met in Granville and had stayed behind did not seem much like fighters. But Roy knew Mr. Wilcox was an ex-soldier and, although he was getting on in years, the man was no weakling.

Roy had also grown fond of young Bob Higgins. It seemed longer but only seven days had passed since Bob rode back home with Jon and Matthew's wolf, Bandit. Remembering the bloody furrow in the boy's shoulder, Roy worried if the kid was able to hoist a rifle in self-defense yet.

Matthew lay as rigid as a board. He also tried to calculate Top Hat's head start and wondered how many boys were riding in with him. Granville was small; only fifty-seven souls within the town limits and another forty or fifty citizens in the outlying area. If his enemy rode into town with a whole gang behind him, Jon and the deputies would be hard-pressed to keep the gang at bay.

He tried to wipe his memory clear of Top Hat with little success; the man's cold, black eyes stared at him through his closed eyelids and his high, girlish voice tittered in his ear. The last thing Matthew saw before slipping into a nightmare-ridden slumber was the sharp-edged gleam of Top Hat's oversized bowie knife, causing him to awake with a startled gasp in the early gray light of dawn.

Long before the sun cleared the treetops, Matthew and Roy rode swiftly out of the mountains, reaching the flatlands by noon. After about an hour, Matthew pulled up short, lifted his nose and muttered, "Do you smell that?"

Roy looked around in confusion. "Smell what, Boss?" Then his eyes got big and he said, "I do! That's smoke, isn't it?"

Matthew nodded. "The wind is following us but, every once in a while, I get a whiff. Something ahead of us is on fire! Let's go!"

The two men nudged their horses and took off at a slow canter. The wind had picked up and big, mushroom-shaped clouds were gathering to the west like a sullen band of hoodlums. To make matters worse, the day's heat was succumbing to the moisture in the air, sweating the horse's necks and causing the men's clothes to stick to their bodies like wet shrouds.

They saw a promonotory about a mile ahead and—squinting at the red and gray rocks—Matthew thought they were moving. Yet knowing that notion was loco did not stop the chill of fear that sizzled through his bloodstream.

"You see that?" Roy asked, even as Matthew reined his horse to a stop and drew his uncle's telescope out of the saddlebag.

Staring at the rocks, he realized they were not moving but at least a hundred crows and buzzards perched on them were. As Matthew watched, a fight broke out and they could hear the bird's carnivorous screeches.

Knowing that birds like these usually congregated at a kill site, Matthew sighed and put the telescope away. "Looks like there's something dead up ahead, Roy."

Roy nodded tersely and said, "Damn it...we'd better go see."

They approached quickly but cautiously. If the

birds fought over a dead cow, they would ignore it and be on their way. However, if it was a dead person, the lawmen were obliged to stop and either bury the body or carry it into town for a proper Christian burial. Whatever awaited them was hidden by the rocks.

The birds muttered and moaned but did not fly away as Matthew and Roy walked their horses around the stony outcropping.

"Aw, Jesus..." Roy gagged, almost falling off his horse in shock at what met their eyes. Matthew felt nausea climb up in his throat as he counted the dead bodies piled by a smoking fire.

A man, two women and four children lay naked in the sweltering sun. Their throats had been slashed and each victim wore a bloody bib crawling with flies. One of the women was elderly but the other was young; it was obvious to the lawmen that she and at least two of the children had been raped before the knife took their lives. Blood painted their thighs and stained the little boy's bottom red in the garish sunlight. Feeling murderous rage fill his chest, Matthew breathed through his mouth to stifle the stench that filled the air.

The flies rose and fell in black waves. Two oxen lay dead in their traces by a smoking ruin that was once a covered wagon; the tarp covering it was nothing but charred rags now flapping bleakly. A small burro was splay-legged by the back of the wagon, its head and neck blackened and leathery from the flames that killed it. Dresses, petticoats, men's britches, cookware, old newspapers, tack, farm implements...all signs of living were strewn about like rubbish.

Staring at the man spread-eagled on the ground, Matthew saw that he held a sheaf of money notes in his hand.

The man had tried to give this money—probably all he had—to the ones who threatened him and his family. But Matthew knew this was a message from Top Hat for, staring past the body on the ground, the sheriff saw a battered hat hanging on a stick placed close to the fire. It was filthy and skewed yet had once been handsome headgear before this villain carried out his worst work; a beaver-skin stovepipe like the one Abraham Lincoln wore was now a symbol of slaughter.

The rage in Matthew's chest burst out of his mouth in an uncontrollable roar and his horse skipped in place again, unsure of what posed the biggest threat: the bodies on the ground; the birds that thrashed and whined like a single entity; or the rider it carried.

Suddenly, a lone coyote ran out from under the burned-out wagon where it had sought refuge and had nowhere else to go but straight ahead. It zipped past Matthew's horse and the nervous animal finally succumbed to fear, rearing up with a squeal of alarm.

Matthew—who was just about to step down to the ground—found himself flying through the air and landing hard on a heavy steel anvil. He heard his ribs break and cried out in dismay even as all his breath whooshed out of his lungs. His cry cut off in a strangled yelp and he lay broken and bleeding on the ground.

He saw swirling whimsies of light and his ears rang like a church bell but when he turned his head to look over at Roy, Matthew came face to face with the dead boy who had met his end at Top Hat's hand.

The boy was close to the same age he was when he had run afoul of the criminal and but for the grace of God, he could have been raped and ruined just like this young innocent with ginger hair and lifeless blue eyes.

"Sheriff! Are you busted up bad?" Roy leaned over him and Matthew turned his head away from the dead boy's gaze.

Matthew grimaced in pain and commenced to checking his own mortal coil. He moved his fingers and toes, lifted both legs and shook his head gently back and forth. Sighing in relief, he knew that he was not paralyzed but the agony in his ribs and lower back was excruciating.

Glancing one last time at the little boy's face, he said, "I will survive but this burial is going to have to wait. I hate to leave these folks like this but the job has just become too much for me."

Staring at the wagon, Matthew saw that its wheels seemed undamaged. Gasping, he said, "Roy hitch two of the horses, please. Looks like I'm going to need a lift into town."

THE WORLD IS A STAGE

ROY HELPED MATTHEW TO HIS FEET AND LED HIM toward a wood stump set away from the fire. The sheriff gritted his teeth against the pain but, even though they walked slowly, the gorge rose up in his throat until he finally bent over and vomited on some nearby sagebrush.

"You got at least a couple of busted ribs, Sheriff, and you're cut up too," Roy muttered as he led a trembling Matthew to the stump.

"Reckon you're right, Roy. There is a medical kit in my saddlebags...could you fetch it for me?" Roy was already walking toward Matthew's horse. The gelding had wandered off a ways after he threw his rider and now eyed the approaching deputy with distrust.

"Whoa there, son...whoa," he crooned and the horse settled down, taking a mouthful of prairie grass. Roy rummaged around, found the medical kit and almost stumbled when his boots got tangled up in a long, white petticoat on the ground.

Staring down at the offending garment, Roy pondered for a moment and then picked it up before moving to Matthew's side. The sheriff was sitting up straight but his head was laid back on his shoulders. Face to the sun, Matthew wore a little smile and he murmured, "I've come up with an idea, Roy."

"Oh, yeah?" Roy asked, handing the sheriff a pinch of ground poppy powder. "Well, why don't you fill me in while I see what's what with this wound of yours?"

Roy peeled off Matthew's vest and pulled his shirt over his head; the sheriff hissed with pain as the sticky red thing stuck to the cut on his back.

The deputy sat on his heels and whistled. "Holy shit, Matthew! I don't think you could have found a worse place to fall off your horse if you tried!"

"Alright, Roy. Point taken. What's the verdict?"

Roy splashed some water from his canteen down Matthew's back, trying to wash the blood and dirt away from a six-inch tear on the man's lower ribcage.

"Oh, the cut is fairly minor. More of a deep scrape than anything. I would guess two or three ribs are broken." Matthew gasped as Roy probed the area. "Just let me clean it as much as possible and then wrap you up tight." Handing Matthew the petticoat, he added, "Do you think you could tear this thing into strips for me?"

When Roy was done, Matthew stood up feeling as

though he was wearing a corset but he could breathe now without wanting to weep with agony.

Roy packed up the medical kit and put it back in his saddlebags while Matthew pulled on his heavy gloves and started knocking away pieces of the wagon's bonnet hoops. Although the potent medicine had taken some of the edge off the pain in his ribs, he moved gingerly and what he could not remove with a mallet, Roy kicked away with his boots.

Then the two men emptied the wagon of the previous owner's personal effects and filled it up with their own belongings. They also wrestled two large wooden crates of china and silverware into the bed; their saddles, gear, ammunition and guns took up the rest of the space.

Matthew was panting with exhaustion and Roy made him a comfortable pallet behind the makeshift barricade.

"Boss, you're a Tom turkey. That's a fact, but I can't take them bandits all by myself. Why don't you lie down and get some rest while I drive this wagon into town?"

Matthew nodded. "Sounds good although I'm not tired. I'll just sit up against these blankets and show you the alternate route into Granville. I'm pretty sure it's about fifteen miles north of here."

"Okay, Boss…here, let me help you." After heaving Sheriff Wilcox into the wagon, Roy lifted his long, gingham skirt in a curtsy, tipped his sunbonnet and hopped onto the driver's bench.

Three hours later, Matthew and Roy crouched on the crest of a small hill and gazed down into the streets of Granville. There were only two streets and nine buildings that made up Matthew's hometown: the sheriff's office; the livery; a restaurant/bakery; two saloons; the laundry/bathhouse; two churches; and the mercantile/post office.

There was a smattering of houses on the east end of town and a large livestock barn and corral at the west entrance. Matthew could not see anyone on the streets except for two men who seemed to be walking back and forth on guard or sentry duty. Even without looking properly, Matthew could tell that his town was besieged.

He got up and walked back to the wagon, fishing around for Jon's telescope. Every step he took and every breath that filled his lungs sent bolts of pain throughout his body but there was no helping that now. He needed to get a good look before he committed himself or his deputy to a course of action.

Walking slowly back to where Roy hid in some high weeds, Matthew knelt by his side. Glassing slowly over the entire town, he now saw the men patrolling the boardwalk on Main Street, plus four others stationed at each end.

He paused as something else caught his attention. Aiming the telescope high, Matthew's breath caught in his throat as he spied four bodies hanging on the high crosspieces of an archway leading into the livestock yard. "Goddammit," he moaned softly.

"What is it, Matthew?" Roy whispered.

"Hold on a minute," Matthew replied as he took in the awful sight. Christopher Rundell, the grocer; Archie Almquist, the cobbler; little Maggie, the baker's daughter; and Deputy Murray Kotes were all hanging by the neck in front of the municipal barn.

It looked like Top Hat had raped and slit the throat of the young girl...her long skirt and apron were covered in blood. This was nothing more than insult added to injury and Matthew could almost see red tongues of fury flare up in his peripheral vision. Turning away before he broke down and wept in sorrow and pity, he handed the telescope to Roy who began to swear in shared rage.

"Hey, isn't that your wolf?" he asked, passing the eyeglass back to the sheriff.

Matthew seized the telescope and searched for his pet. Then he saw that it was Maggie's...a mongrel named Muffin that had adopted the girl last winter when she fed him scraps from the bakery during the long snows. The scruffy, old dog crept up to the wooden fence rails and stared up at her body where she hung by the neck about six feet above.

Lifting his muzzle, Muffin howled a lament into the gray, hazy sky. Then one of Top Hat's crew threw a handful of rocks at the dog. A stone hit its mark, Muffin yelped, and took off running back down the street.

Gazing at the wide barn doors, Matthew thought he saw movement in the darkened interior; he made a slight adjustment and saw a flash of red. Iris appeared in the doorway and yelled something at the two men standing guard. It was obvious she was hurling some insult or other because one of the men—a scar faced Mexican with silver Conchos sewn up and down his pants legs and vest—lifted his rifle and aimed it in her direction.

"No!" Matthew breathed as sweat beaded his brow. Then he saw hands seize the widow Imes from behind and pull her backward out of sight.

Heart hammering in fear, Matthew finally understood that he was in love with Iris and had been for years. But there had always been too many things in the way for his heart to let loose to hers...his burning need for revenge, guilt, and worry over his childhood friend Marie. Yet having seen the fiery beauty stand up to the gangsters and almost get shot only served to remind him that he had more to fight for than mere vengeance.

Turning to Roy he said, "We need to get a move on. Are you still up for this?"

Roy nodded. "Hell yes, Matthew. Goddamn their hides! This comes to an end now!"

The men crouched in the weeds about a quarter of a mile from the edge of town. At the foot of the hill ran a tiny stream with a handmade wooden bridge where many folks went to picnic or fish. More importantly, the little bridge was concealed behind a stand of weeping willows. Matthew knew, if he had to, he could shoot any one of the bandits from that distance.

Meanwhile, Roy planned on doing the same from the other side of town. All he had to do was make his way from here to there in one piece. That was why both Matthew and his deputy wore dresses and bonnets. Though Matthew was too tall and muscular to pull off the acting job very well, Roy was a smaller man and just over 165 pounds.

With any luck, Roy would saunter over the bridge with his umbrella and reticule in hand, looking for all the world like a lady out for a stroll. Yet too much depended upon good timing and Matthew's heart pounded in his chest as Roy strapped another rifle to his left leg and his two pistols under a dirty gray shawl.

Both men carried every weapon they owned tied to their bodies and hidden under the women's clothes. Matthew would go down off the hillside first and scout the area so that Roy could make his way across the footbridge and into the residential area of town.

"You ready?" Matthew whispered.

Nodding, Roy said, "Good luck, Sheriff."

"Thanks, Roy. I'll watch your back."

Then Matthew turned and made his way slowly down the hill. Although the little incline was too far away for any of the bandits to get off a shot, he prayed no one could actually see him and give the game away. He had no doubt he and his deputy could kill a few outlaws if it came to a shoot-out but Matthew wanted to take *all* of them out of commission forever and free the hostages before dispatching Top Hat for good.

Reaching the bottom of the hill, he crouched in the

meadow grass about twenty-five feet away from the creek. His heart thundered in his chest and he waited for a bullet to come whizzing by or a warning shout to rise in the still afternoon air but, so far, it seemed as if his presence had gone undetected. He crawled on his belly the rest of the way until he knew the tree's fronds hid him. After a few moments, Matthew turned around and gave Roy the all-go signal.

The Spokane County deputy stepped out from where he had been hiding and strolled down the hill as if he didn't have a care in the world. If Matthew weren't so sad and nervous, he would have laughed at Roy's antics. Perhaps the young deputy made a study of women and how they walked as Matthew knew that, to anyone who didn't know better, Roy would be mistaken for a young girl returning home from some outing or tryst by the river. The gingham skirt he wore swung enticingly and the parasol over his left shoulder twirled gaily in the sunshine.

As Matthew waited for a shot to ring out, Roy strolled across the bridge and up the pathway that led into town. Then he darted quickly behind one of the nicer houses and let himself in the back door.

Matthew finally allowed himself a grin; Roy had just succeeded in bringing their arsenal into Granville. Now all he had to do was crawl through the high grass and join his friend in the battle over Matthew's home-town and the people he had sworn to protect.

29

A SAD REUNION

MATTHEW COMMENCED TO CRAWLING ON HIS BELLY. HIS ribs pained him and he wished he had taken another pinch of the poppy but knew that he needed to keep his wits about him. Just a little too much medicine would dull his senses and make him draw too slowly or miss entirely if push came to shove.

He was almost to the fence line of Madeline Forsyth's house when he heard masculine voices. He froze, pressing himself into the ground and listening to the men speak. It was remarkable how well their voices carried in the still afternoon air. Perhaps it was because the usual clamor of everyday life was absent or maybe it was the storm front moving in from the west that made every word the men said carry.

Peering through the weeds, Matthew saw two men pause in front of the house. They had stopped walking and stood on the road rolling cigarettes. The sheriff knew, if either one of them glanced in his direction, he would be spotted. Out in the meadow—among the weeds and rocks—his beige bonnet and long skirts might have blended into the landscape as long as he did not move. Where he lay now, though, his clothes stood out like a sore thumb.

Matthew took his pistol in hand and readied himself to shoot. But the two men turned away and stared back down the road; their conversation made his heart skip a beat.

"Boss is feeling pretty bloody, eh?" one of the men asked.

The other agreed. "Yeah. Glad to be away from him right now, truth be told."

"What do you think this whole thing is about anyway? This town is poor. Don't even have a bank!"

To which the second man replied, "Oh, I don't reckon this is about money. I hear this is a blood feud. Boss says as soon as the sheriff comes back, we'll kill him and torch the whole damn town."

Matthew bared his teeth in fury. *We will just see about that!* He thought, rising to his feet in order to run behind the house. The pain of it made him see stars for a second and then he ran in a crouch until he clung to the clapboards by the back door. He was in a vulnerable position as, if the crooks decided to use the privy, he would be found and a shoot-out would ensue.

He also knew he could not open the screen door and go inside the house because it screeched like a banshee. Therefore, he slowly made his way around

and crept through the yard until he was on the opposite corner of the home from where the men loitered.

Keeping one eye on the outhouse and another
trained on the road in front, Matthew waited. Glancing
to his left, he saw a curtain twitch in the house where
Roy sought shelter. He wanted to reconnoiter with the
deputy but knew the two bandits needed to leave
before he dared abandon his post.

A few tension-filled moments passed when wasps
from a papery nest in the rafters above his head
explored his bonnet but then Matthew saw the men
walking away toward the middle of town. Staring into
the distance as a few drops of rain from the incoming
storm dotted the dust and dry grass under his feet,
Matthew saw them meet up with two other strangers
in front of his office.

All four men turned as one, studied something in
front of the sheriff's office and then parted company.
The two who had paused for a smoke went west, the
two others stepped back inside the building. Knowing
that now was as safe a time as any, Matthew fell to his
knees and crawled on the ground behind a low picket
fence to within ten feet of where Roy hid.

There were a few peach and apple trees in the yard,
some of them heavy with fruit. Matthew wriggled
under the pickets and found himself squirming
through fallen, overripe peaches. The pulp squished
under his hands and stained his skirts as he made his
way to the back stoop.

Looking up, he saw Roy standing just inside the

door. "Hurry up, Boss! They're heading this way again!"

Matthew ran into the house. Once inside and blinking through the gloom, a happy sight met his eyes. Young Bob Higgins stood by the cold woodstove, wringing his oversized hat in his hands. Bandit whined happily, stood up on his back legs and showered Matthew's face with wet licks.

"Bandit," Matthew whispered as he hugged the animal, "you're a good boy. A very good boy." Looking over at Bob, he said, "It's good to see you, too."

Bob looked miserable and bent his hat in his hands again. "Sir, I got some bad news."

Matthew's glad heart shriveled a little in his chest. He held his hands up though and murmured, "Hold up a minute with your news, Bob. I got to get out of these clothes."

Roy had taken off the women's clothing and Matthew did the same, trying to avoid the peachy pulp as much as possible. Shawl, bonnet and skirt flew into a pile in the corner of the room where Bandit followed, sniffing at the mess.

Matthew knew from the look on the young deputy's face that someone had died but the sheriff thought he already knew what had happened...he had seen the dead bodies hanging by the stockyard. He went to a large water pitcher and poured himself a cup before sitting at the table with a painful wince.

"Okay, let's hear it," Matthew said.

The young man's face twisted in fear and his mouth opened and closed a couple of times before he could

speak. The sheriff glanced over at Roy in consterna-
tion- who stared back at him in pity.   Matthew
suddenly understood that he did not know the whole
truth.

"Sit down and tell me what happened."

Bob gulped and pulled out a chair. "Sir, I hate to say
it but your Uncle Jon and his wife are both dead." The
young man trembled at the look that came over his
sheriff's face.

Matthew felt the blood drain from his head and for
one breathless moment, he feared he would faint and
fall. Unwanted tears filled his eyes even as a terrifying
wave of fury filled his heart. Wiping the moisture away
from his cheeks, Matthew whispered, "How did this
happen?"

Bob told both lawmen what had taken place two
nights earlier.

"Sheriff, I stayed with Mr. Wilcox and his wife for
five days. They were good to me and helped me with
my injury. I woulda still been there but for the fact that
the Burnsides wanted to go on into Spokane Falls on
account of Mrs. Burnside's daughter is having
a baby…"

Bob poured a drink of water from the pitcher.
"Anyway, the Burnsides asked if I could come here and
keep an eye out on things—harvest the fruit on those
trees out back and feed their chickens while they were
gone. Well, I was happy to do it and get out from
underfoot at your uncle's place so I moved my kit over
here and the Burnsides took off to Spokane Falls. Later

that same night, I was sleeping here on the couch and I thought I heard a ruckus in the chicken coop. I figured a raccoon or a fox was up to no good, so I grabbed my shotgun and went outside to look."

His eyes big with the remembered horror, he continued, "That decision saved my life, sir, cuz no sooner did I step into the coop than a bunch of men came bustin' in the front door of the house! They tore things up some and made a mess but mainly, I think, they were lookin' for hostages. Lucky for me, I guess, because once I heard 'em I ducked down inside the roost and waited for them to leave."

Bob gazed up at Matthew's face. "I crept out a little later and hid behind some tall scrub to get an eye on what was happening. I saw everybody being herded out of their houses and led down the street at gunpoint to the livestock barn. Then I saw five men drag your uncle and his wife out the front door of their—I mean —your house, sir." He gulped and shook his head as though denying the images in his mind's eye he knew to be true.

"Oh, sir, it was awful!" he cried. "I don't rightly know how they got the drop on your uncle the way they did, but four men held him down while the others took turns…" Bob covered his face with shaking hands. "Oh, don't make me say it, sir!"

"That's alright, Bob. I get the picture," Matthew murmured through frozen, grief-stricken lips.

"Anyways, after they finished, they killed poor Margie and then our town folk were forced to stay and watch what came next." Bob gasped. "I think that one of those skunks—I'm pretty sure it was that gawddam Top Hat—was trying to rape your uncle but it took six of those outlaws to subdue him. I think they finally just gave up on that notion 'cuz it was too much trouble. But it didn't stop Top Hat from stepping up from behind and cutting your uncle's throat with that big knife of his!"

Matthew's whole body recoiled in horror as Bob went on to describe how the next day he had watched as the gang members left town only to return a few hours later with their friends and neighbors trussed up against their will and thrown in the barn with the other captives.

As Bob relayed his news as carefully and compassionately as he could, Matthew was lost in his own memories. He recalled waking up from his own kidnapping and seeing his father's face staring down at him, only this man was dark and much thinner with kindly, green eyes.

He remembered how hard Jonathon had worked to raise Matthew as his own and the deep but quiet love and respect his uncle had shown him over the years. He recalled his uncle's fear when he realized that Matthew's heart was set on destroying the criminal known as Top Hat and, finally, Matthew accepted the fact the he was to blame for his aunt and uncle's deaths.

Bob stammered in dismay at the subtle but fearful change that came over the sheriff's face as Matthew's heart turned to stone.

30

"LIFE IS BUT A DREAM"

THE THREE MEN STAYED UP LATE TALKING ABOUT THE preceding day's events, the outlaws and the almost magical reappearance of Matthew's wolf. Bandit had been staying with Jon and Margaret when the outlaws overcame the couple but had somehow managed to escape without injury.

That Bandit was an escape artist, Matthew had no doubt. Still, it was remarkable since Bob thought that over eight men had busted into the house, guns roaring. Reaching down to scratch the animal between his ears, Matthew knew it was nothing short of a miracle that his pet panted happily by his side.

They also made plans. Matthew knew something about the large barn where the prisoners were held captive; Davey O'Donnell and his brother Joseph had made a sort of sinkhole outside of the back. Normally, the barn and livestock pens were sparsely populated but this was not a big town and most through-traffic flowed westerly into the larger Spokane Falls area. Occasionally, however, the stalls and pens would be filled to overflowing along with the natural by-products of their guests. That is when the two brothers opened a small hatch at the rear of the barn and shoveled manure into the cesspool.

Unfortunately, when the temperatures were high or there was a weather inversion, the stink in the hole rose into the air, filling the town with toxic fumes. Over the years, numerous complaints had landed on the sheriff's desk saying things like *deal with those damn Irish stinkers or we will!*

Finally, just last year, Matthew had convinced the stable owners to stop polluting the town's air supply by commissioning a poop wagon to stop by once a week, collect the manure and drive by the local farms and ranches to drop off free fertilizer for their gardens.

The cesspool had been covered over with dirt and was just starting to settle into the ground again but Matthew still knew where the little hatch was. Unfortunately, he would have to wade through shit to get to it.

The men grew still as, once again, they heard the sounds of footsteps on the road. Matthew crept to the window and peered outside. All three of them crouched down with their hands on their guns and waited in tense silence as the outlaws paused in front of the house and then turned around and proceeded back the way they came.

A few minutes later, after finalizing their plans,

Matthew lay down on a pallet on the floor. He was exhausted and the pain in his ribs and lower back made a very long and sad day seem even more taxing. Hearing the two deputies do the same, Matthew closed his eyes and fell into a dream-filled slumber.

In the dream, he was fourteen years old and sitting at the kitchen table with his Uncle Jon and grandfather, Peter. They had found a little chalkboard and were trying to teach the bored and ailing Matthew about history and literature. He was fidgeting anxiously, and kept peeking out the windows at the buttery yellow sunshine and the blue skies that were still out of reach to him in his convalescence.

Jon had promised that Matthew would be allowed outdoors just as soon as his strength returned but the boy despaired of that day ever coming again. Peter, whose love of the classics sometimes tested his son's patience as much as Matthew's, was droning on about one of Shakespeare's plays, the tragic romance of Romeo and Juliet.

Jon had grinned as Matthew was literally nodding off and said, "Father, it looks like your pupil is asleep."

Peter stared at the boy for a moment before closing the leather tome.

"Well," he murmured. "Shakespeare is not every-one's cup of tea."

Matthew had awoken with a startled snort and said, "I'm sorry, Grandfather! I didn't mean to doze off."

Peter gazed at him fondly and replied, "That's alright, my boy. I think you might like what your uncle has planned next. Did your papa ever tell you about the Trojan horse?"

Wracking his brains, Matthew finally shook his head. "I thought I'd heard about every kind of horse but I guess I missed that one."

Peter grinned and said, "Well, this is a different kind of horse alright." Getting to his feet, Peter added, "I am going to see if there are any more of those tarts in the pantry." Then he walked out the door into the hallway while Jon sat in the vacant chair and proceeded to teach history—and the art of war—to his foster son.

Matthew woke up five hours later with a smile on his face. Checking the pocket watch that hung from a fob made out of a long-dead Negro's long hair, he nodded in satisfaction; it was one o'clock in the morning. Getting to his feet, he shook both of the deputies awake and whispered, "It's time to get going."

Roy and Bob rose and donned their gun belts. Although they had already checked, they counted their bullets again and tested the blades of their knives. Bandit sat watching, his golden eyes gleaming in the shadows as Matthew opened a jar of peaches and cut slices of bread from one of Mrs. Burnside's loaves.

The men finished their breakfast and Matthew said, "Are you ready?"

Both Roy and Bob nodded mutely and the sheriff said, "I won't hold it against either one of you if you would rather hightail it into Spokane Falls. We could use the extra help and this will be a dangerous day."

Both men stared back at him with offended eyes and Matthew smiled. "Okay, follow me."

Checking one last time to make sure the guards were nowhere near, they stepped out into the night. All three lawmen bent low and moved through town toward the barn. As they drew nearer to the large structure, they could see tall flames lick up from a bonfire in front of it.

Pressing themselves into a low crouch, Matthew and his deputies approached the cesspool. They were in the shadows, but two of the outlaws who were on guard duty seemed to be wide- awake and well into their cups. The sounds of rough laughter rose into the air and Matthew knew this must be done quickly or all his well-laid plans would be for naught.

Stepping down into the cesspool, Matthew held his breath. With any luck, he wouldn't break the earthen crust and fall through to the old shit below. Gingerly making his way across the dirt and weeds, he almost made it to the back of the barn when his boot broke the mud and he sank almost to his hips into the sewage.

Swearing to himself, he slogged through the offal and made it to a natural incline in the pool floor closer to the barn. His boots scrambled for purchase, then clinging to the shit-covered ground and the bottom of the barn walls, he pursed his lips and started to whistle a soft tune.

Many years ago, Matthew had gone to Spokane Falls with his uncle and grandfather to hear the renowned opera singer, Jenny Lind, also known as the

Swedish Nightingale. She had sung many songs but the one he remembered best was from *Der Frieschutz*. As the hair on the back of his neck had risen in awe at the woman's beautiful soprano voice, he recalled glancing to his left and seeing the look of wonder on Iris Imes's face as she sat four chairs down from him next to her husband. She had caught his eye and smiled.

Now he hoped she also remembered that song well for those were the notes he whistled into the wallboards of the barn. His deputies were stationed on either side of him and ready to open fire on the bandits if they came around the back to relieve themselves or to investigate. *So far, so good,* Matthew thought as he heard the men out front singing their own unmelodic and bawdy tunes.

He whistled again and suddenly heard a whispered shuffle on the other side of the barn wall. There was a light knocking noise and Matthew grinned when he heard Iris's sleepy whisper, "Mattie, is that you?"

"Yes, it's me," he answered. "Iris, you need to do something for me. This piece of wall in front of you is a hatch. Davey and Joseph nailed it shut a while back but someone in there should be able to pry it open. Can you do that for me?"

"You bet I can," came her grim reply. "I'll do it myself if I have to."

Matthew heard more startled voices beyond the wall and soon he saw a knife slide out from a cut in the wood about twelve inches from his nose. Leaning backwards, he almost fell into the cesspool but managed to catch his balance in time. Glancing over at Roy, Matthew saw the deputy roll his eyes in nervous amusement.

Then he saw a couple of knives and a crowbar make an appearance. In almost complete silence, the small wooden door fell away onto the ground. Matthew picked it up and laid it close to the hole in the barn wall.

Matthew's boots and pant legs were slick with sewer muck and he knew he must stink to high heaven but that did not stop Iris from grinning at him happily and leaning out the little door to plant a kiss on his mouth.

"Finally, you're back," she said. "It's about time!"

Matthew saw Iris's two children and most of the town's citizens staring at him with bleak and weary faces.

He smiled at the townsfolk he had come to love and whispered, "Let me in there...we have work to do."

31

A SUBTERFUGE

Iris backed away and two sets of strong, masculine hands reached through the small hole in the wall and seized Matthew by the shoulders. He heard muffled grunts as he was hauled into the chute and, although the pain was spectacular, he managed to squirm the rest of the way into the barn. Then Davey O'Donnell and Dish, the blacksmith, turned back to the hole and hauled his deputies in as well.

The captives crowded around Matthew, whispering words of thanks. They tried to grab his hand in welcome but still looked over their shoulders toward the front of the barn in fear.

"It's good to be back, people, but we have a lot of work to do before we're out of this fix," he said softly. "Let's go behind that stall there so if one of those bastards comes looking, they won't see us."

Nodding in understanding, the men, women and

children crouched and sat behind the high wooden walls of one of the larger stalls. Matthew, Roy and Bob stood in front of them and emptied their persons of all the guns and knives they carried. The men who had been taken prisoner looked excited and hopeful for the first time as they saw the gleaming, loaded weapons placed before them on the straw-covered ground.

"Go ahead and get one for each of you, okay?" Matthew watched as his neighbors armed themselves with grim resolution. A couple of women also grabbed guns and knives. At first, Matthew thought he should stop them and then reconsidered. He knew for certain that both of these women were crack shots and, in light of what he was about to ask of them now, he wanted women who were able to handle themselves in a fight.

After all the guns and knives he and his deputies had smuggled into the barn were confiscated, he asked the people to sit down again and listen to his plan. At first, there was some protest but not too much. These people knew they were in a tight fix and at least Matthew's idea would help keep most of the women and children safe in the hours to come.

Twenty minutes later, most of the women, children and oldsters were sneaking away out of the poop chute into the darkness. Iris was hesitant over being asked to go but special emphasis was put on her children's welfare, her own fighting abilities, her horses that were still at home on her ranch, and the large barn that would serve as a hostel for the escaped refugees.

Matthew took one of her arms as she prepared to wriggle through the chute. Pulling her away from the others, he looked into her eyes and said, "Iris, I ..." Suddenly, he was at a loss for words. He had carried bitterness and retribution in his heart for so long he barely knew how to express his love for her.

Iris stared up at him and smiled. Placing her hand on his cheek, she whispered, "Oh Mattie, I know. I love you, too." Then, despite the eyes that watched them and heedless of society's censure, she stood on her toes and placed her lips on his.

Matthew was acutely aware they were being observed but he did not care. He wrapped his long arms around Iris's body and kissed her back with all the passion and promise his future could allow. There was a good possibility that he wouldn't survive the upcoming conflict and he wanted this brave and lovely woman to know what was in his heart if he was killed.

As their kiss lingered and the heat between them grew, Iris rejoiced. She had loved her husband but she was ready for this young man to take his place in her heart. Tears welled up in her eyes, though, for she was no fool. Matthew was taking a huge risk with his own life in order to save her and the rest of the people in town. Knowing this might be the last time she saw him alive, she clung to him a moment longer and then stepped away.

"Well," she said. "I better go and join the others."

Matthew stared at her and said, "Stay safe, Iris. And

if any one of those crooks comes after you, shoot to kill!"

She nodded. "Oh, believe me, I will." She searched his face one last time, gathered up her skirts, and slithered out of the chute to join the others running away in the night.

"Are you sure about this, Boss?" Bob asked as he prepared to follow Iris.

"Yes, Bob. I need your help keeping the others safe. Remember first light and no closer than 400 yards."

"Got it, sir," Bob said and stuck out his hand to shake. "Good luck, Sheriff."

Matthew shook the young man's hand and wished him good luck as well. Then Bob slid out the chute and went his own way while the others headed to the safety of Iris Imes's barn. Matthew felt certain that Top Hat meant no harm to the prisoners until the outlaw spotted the sheriff.

Turning back to those who had stayed behind, he smiled in satisfaction. They were now a total of eight armed and very pissed-off men. Subduing and murdering a bunch of unarmed and defenseless citizens was one thing; trying that with people who were enraged and loaded for bear was quite another. Still, according to Dish, Top Hat's gang included at least a dozen murderous savages who were all good with a gun.

Sighing, Matthew thought, the odds are bad, but many members of this outlaw gang are about to meet their maker today.

A half hour later—as Matthew, Roy, Dish and Granville Deputy Evan McCauley slipped back out of the chute and made their way stealthily through the high brush and weeds on the west side of the barn— Lanny Combs and Henry Mulloy swayed on their feet and drank the stout, black coffee Ike Nelson had brought them from the saloon.

Their hearts were still thundering in their chests. The first thing the boss's lieutenant had done was materialize like some sort of a spook out of the shadows and hold them at gunpoint. Then he had snarled at them like a rabid beast.

"Top Hat didn't hire you two to get drunk on your asses. If this is all the good you are on guard duty, I might as well put you in the ground right now!"

"No, sir!" Both men had blanched with alarm. They were new to the gang and scared of Top Hat and his right-hand man. Both of those men were about half crazy with a dangerous glint in their eyes that informed the two novices that these particular outlaws boasted more than their fair share of meanness.

Nelson glared at them, then held out a coffeepot and said, "Throw that hooch away and fill up on this. I'll be back at dawn and if you two are not as sober as church mice, you'll answer for it!"

He turned and went up the street toward the saloon where Top Hat had taken residence. The young guards watched Ike Nelson walk away and then hustled to do as ordered. Throwing away the rotgut, they filled their cups with coffee and stared, trembling, into the darkness.

Just as soon as they did, Dish and Evan slipped across the road and ran to hide behind the bathhouse. They would make their way up onto the roof and cover the front of the barn once all hell broke loose.

Matthew and Roy watched the criminals and then looked at each other. The way was clear—at least for a few minutes—until the pair of roaming guards approached from the other end of town. Matthew took his slingshot out of his pocket, took careful aim and hit one of them on the back of his head. The man fell as straight as a board and landed on his face in the dirt.

No sooner did the sheriff let loose of his rock, Roy was moving fast. He came up behind the other guard, dealing him a crushing blow with the hilt of his knife. In the course of less than five minutes, both of the criminals were out cold, gagged, and hauled into the bushes.

Matthew knew this was the most hazardous and time-sensitive part of his plan but he grinned when two more men from his hometown came flying around from behind the barn, stripped the outlaws of their coats and hats, plucked their firearms out of their hands and then stood by the burn-barrel sipping hot coffee.

Two more men hauled the outlaws away as Matthew and Roy ran across the street and around to the alley behind the bathhouse, the restaurant and the sheriff's office. Matthew's heart filled with dread at what he was about to do but it was as if his uncle had whispered instructions into his ear.

He looked at his pocket watch again; they had made good time. It was 3:30 in the morning, though, and he still had work to do before first light. He had no Trojan horse in which to hide but there was another way and he intended to do it now. Top Hat was about to find out what messing with Matthew Wilcox really meant.

32

A TERRIBLE GAMBLE

IT WAS 4:20 IN THE MORNING OF AUGUST 21, 1885. IKE Nelson stepped out of the saloon and stood on the boardwalk taking in the cool, misty air and sipping tepid coffee from a tin cup. Mourning doves sang their sad, inquisitive hellos…who-who-who?

Ike couldn't help but wonder that himself. Who had he become by hitchin' his wagon to Top Hat? He had heard some years ago that Top Hat was a fair shot and not afraid to take what he wanted from anyone. He had seemed like a good candidate for partnership, especially after a run of bad luck and the ever-growing, long arm of the law had almost stranded him in a hangman's noose in South Dakota.

Now, though, Nelson was becoming more and more convinced that he was entangled in the clinging, sticky, web-like strands of a lunatic spider. Top Hat's mad excesses were becoming more apparent and his motivations less clear as time went by. The gang leader no longer seemed interested in money or any kind of capital gain. Instead, he seemed to want to strike and murder for the sheer fun of practicing his perversions upon his victims.

Ike spat upon the dirt road in front of his boots. Another thing that was really starting to get on his nerves was Top Hat's homosexual tendencies. The dirty louse loved buggering men and little boys, even to death if possible. Ike's lips twisted in scorn. *I might be a bad man,* he thought, *but I ain't no pervert!*

Glancing across the street, Ike studied the body of Jon Wilcox. The man had been placed sitting upright in a straight-backed chair on the porch of the sheriff's office after he finally died. That was two days ago and now he was starting to stink. The flies crawled, buzzed and swarmed around the body and the roaming guards were starting to step off the boardwalk and give the dead man a wide berth in fearful disgust.

It looked to Ike like the man's rigor was starting to fade now; the body was no longer stiff but sagging in his seat and the dried blood on the man's white-starched shirt faded to brown in the early morning light.

The door to the saloon was slightly ajar and Ike heard his companions snoring inside where they had fallen asleep on assorted tables and chairs. *Crazy assholes. Each and every one of 'em,* Ike thought and decided right then, as soon as this caper was finished, he would make himself scarce.

Turning toward the west, Ike saw the two guards by

the barn patrolling back and forth in front of the burn barrel. He grinned... *I got the drop on those two pups and it looks like they heard me loud and clear!*

He was just about to step inside for another cup of coffee when he heard a shout. Staring again at the two men guarding the barn, Ike saw one of them gesturing and jumping up and down in excitement. The barn was about fifty feet down the street and the sun was in his eyes but he could hear one of the men yelling, "Boss, it's the sheriff!"

Ike felt his heart speed up. Finally, Matthew Wilcox was returning to town. *Maybe,* he thought, *we can put this farce behind us and go back to getting rich robbing trains and stagecoaches.* Stepping inside, he walked to where Top Hat was sleeping with his head down on the bar. He shook the man's shoulder and said, "Boss, wake up. The sheriff is coming in."

Top Hat sat up straight, his eyes doing their jittery dance. "How far out?" he asked.

"Oh, a ways yet," Ike said and went over to wake Chollo and Top Hat's personal physician, Levon Smithers.

Top Hat stood up and staggered over to the coffeepot. He had drunk more than he should have the previous night and was suffering for it now. Still, there was a happy smile on his face and, as he drank his coffee, his feet did a little jig.

"Gonna get that fucker," he muttered as he danced. "Gonna show him who is the real boss."

Ike turned away in disgust as the other two men

strapped on their pistols. Then Top Hat spat the last of his beverage into a spittoon and said, "Let's go!"

Top Hat and his lieutenants stepped outside and peered into the rising sun. Sure enough, they saw two men on horseback sitting a few hundred yards away with the sun to their backs. Ike glanced toward the guards by the barn and saw them hunkered down, sighting along the barrels of their rifles at the two riders.

"You got your torches?" Top Hat was hyperventilating with excitement.

Ike stared down at his boots for a moment before nodding his head. Yes, he had killed plenty of men and women since he left his hometown as a young man but never just for the sheer thrill of killing. Top Hat was different though; he was happy to torch all those souls in the barn despite the fact that most of them were women and children with no money.

This was all about some sort of bad blood feud between the gang leader and this Sheriff Wilcox. Ike wanted no part of it but it was too late to change things now. He knew the time for murder was at hand and a little part of his soul turned to ash as he stepped forward with the other criminals to do the dirty deed.

As the outlaws walked toward the barn, they saw one of the distant riders take aim with a rifle. A small puff of dust rose up no more than a foot away from one of their boy's boots.

"Holy shit!" one of the men cried. "Did you see that?

They're hundreds of yards away by my reckoning and they almost got me!"

Top Hat saw both men duck around the backside of the barn and he said, "Remind me to shoot those yellow bastards as soon as this shindig is done."

"I'll be happy to do it myself, Boss," Chollo said as he saw the guards disappear from sight.

Two more gang members who had been on patrol all night came running in their direction. Top Hat pointed at them and screamed, "You two! Go and fire that barn!"

Nodding as they hurried past, they grabbed the torches Top Hat and his lieutenants were holding. Moving swiftly, the men held the kerosene-soaked rags on sticks into the flames of the burn-barrel then threw them into the high windows in front of the barn.

There was a breathless calm and then Ike heard the sounds of agonized screaming coming from inside. Shuddering, he looked for the other pair of guards who had been patrolling the west end of town. Ike knew they were a couple of slackers who liked to take frequent smoke breaks but they should have arrived by now. He turned to look at Top Hat who was hooting with maniacal glee.

Chollo yelled, "Here they come, Boss!"

Then, out of the corner of his eye, Ike saw something that made his blood run cold. The dead man who was parked in front of the sheriff's office—melting in his chair with the stench of death filling the air around him—rose slowly, pulled his pistol out of his gun belt and barked, "Top Hat! Drop your weapons now!"

An hour earlier, Matthew and Roy had carefully eased Jon's decomposing body off the chair and dragged him around behind the office. Moving swiftly, Matthew had undressed his uncle and put on his stinking, blood-stiff clothing. Blinking back tears of sorrow as he covered Jon's nudity with his own clothes, he had muttered an apology under his breath.

Noticing the nasty bruises and cuts on Matthew, Roy whispered, "You sure you're up to this, Sheriff?"

Nodding, Matthew swallowed back the gorge rising up in his throat. "Yes. I can do better in Jon's seat than trying to crawl up on this roof. You better get going, Roy."

The deputy whispered good luck and stepped up on a stump so he could grab a hold of the eaves, then scrambled the rest of the way to the top.

The lawmen had received word that the roaming guards on the west end of town had been knocked unconscious and dragged into the barn to keep the other bandits company. If Dish's estimate was correct, that left six men to deal with: Top Hat, Clarence Dodson (aka Ike Nelson), Chollo, Levon Smithers and the two who had just torched the barn. Matthew smiled grimly. The odds were getting better by the minute.

He tucked his long hair under his uncle's hat, crouched low and moved around to the front of his office, taking Jon's place in the chair on the porch. He had no sooner got himself situated when the man he knew as Clarence Dodson stepped out of the saloon with a cup in his hand.

Matthew's heart burned with rage as he saw the man survey the town as if he owned it. It was all the sheriff could do to keep still as the outlaw turned his way and studied his slumped body with a smile on his face. Flies were returning to investigate the dried blood on his uncle's shirt and he was just about to sneeze when a shout shattered the quiet, early dawn.

Peering through half-closed eyes, Matthew saw Bob and Evan silhouetted on the western horizon. He heard Davey O'Connell call out his lines like a natural-born actor and then saw Dodson step back into the saloon. A few moments later, four men walked out onto the boardwalk. Matthew's heart thundered in his chest as his old nemesis, Top Hat, came into view.

The gang leader was just as stick-thin and ugly as ever with his lank brown hair, buckteeth and wandering, jittery eyes. Matthew wanted nothing more than to drill that man right between the shoulder blades with his Colt pistol but honor—and the legal system—stilled his hand.

He watched as the criminals approached the barn, grinning when it caught fire. Matthew was not a vicious man but too much had happened for him to shed a tear over the fate of the four gangsters burning alive inside the building. He was relieved that he and his men had managed to free the hostages; if he had held any doubts over Top Hat's intentions, they were laid to rest.

Briefly, Matthew felt the weight of sorrow, regret, and his recent injuries bear down on his shoulders like an anvil. A moment later, while the bandit's backs were turned, he stood up and hollered, "Top Hat! Drop your weapons! NOW!"

33

THE SHOWDOWN

"GET DOWN ON YOUR KNEES AND TOSS YOUR WEAPONS behind you!" Matthew snapped. He walked up slowly, keeping one eye on the outlaws and one eye on the two riders in the distance.

"Roy, you want to get the deputies' attention for me, please?" Matthew called out.

"Sure thing, Sheriff," Roy answered from where he crouched on the roof and let out a piercing whistle to signal Bob and Evan that it was safe to come into town. Matthew saw Top Hat flinch with the knowledge that he and his gang were now surrounded.

"Dish, you got a bead on these crooks?" Matthew yelled and the man on the bathhouse roof answered in the affirmative.

"And my brother and I have these arsonists dead to rights, Sheriff!" Davey called from in front of the barn.

Matthew saw Bob and Evan spurring their horses toward town and his shoulders dropped a little in relief. As best as he could tell, the outlaws were under the gun and it was all over but for a hanging once the circuit judge rolled into town.

Looking back down at the four outlaws, he said, "I am not inclined to shoot any of you in the back but if I don't see *all* of your guns at my feet by the count of three…two… one…"

Three pistols and one long, deadly machete joined the pile of weapons on the ground in front of Matthew's boots. He kicked the guns and the knife behind him and looked up at young Bob and Evan as they rode past the burning barn. He smiled and was just about to tell them they had done a good job when a fiery explosion rocked the ground he was standing on and almost burst his eardrums.

Something inside the barn—he would find out later it was a barrel of kerosene the O'Connell brothers kept on hand for heating up shoe-iron—had ignited and went off like a bomb. The fiercely burning building blew up, sending wood as small as lit matchsticks, lathe and gigantic pieces of flaming lumber in every direction at once.

A fireball as big as a house whooshed down the street toward him and Matthew's ears rang with a high-pitched whine. He saw Bob and Evan engulfed in the shrieking inferno; their horses screamed and the sheriff knew that his two deputies and the O'Connell brothers must be dead. He saw Bob and Evan's burning bodies etched in fire as were their horses who reared up in the air—manes and tails aflame—running away and screaming in agony through the black smoke rising from where the barn once stood. Trembling with shock, Matthew looked down at the criminals on the ground in front of him.

He thought the terrifying spectacle had only taken a moment or two but it was long enough that Top Hat had somehow managed to jump up and run off. But the outlaw known as Chollo lie dead on the ground, apparently shot in the back by one of the shooters on the rooftops, and Levon Smithers was sprawled on his back, staring up into the sky with a burning sliver of lumber through his chest.

Ike Nelson, however, sat on in the dirt pointing a Colt pistol in Matthew's face.

"Don't you do it, you skunk!" Roy yelled down from the roof behind Matthew. "I will take your damn head off with this rifle!"

"Yeah, maybe," Ike snarled. "But you will kill your own sheriff if you try!"

Matthew knew Nelson might be right: He stood almost directly between Roy and the outlaw and, even as he watched, Nelson scooted over slightly in the dirt so Matthew's large body covered his own.

Enraged beyond reason, he screamed, "Do it, Roy! Shoot the bastard dead!"

As though in slow motion, he ducked and felt the heat of Roy's bullet as it flew over his uncle's felt hat and saw the slug enter Nelson's forehead. At that same moment, he felt a burning sensation in his left side. Moisture dripped down his pants leg and

Matthew almost wondered if it had started raining again.

He looked up into the gray smoke, trying to get a glimpse of the blue sky overhead. Then he fell as his mind finally registered the fact that, before Nelson had been shot between the eyes, he had managed to get off his own shot.

The man's Army Colt 41 pistol lay smoking on the ground next to the dead hand that held it but the bullet was lodged somewhere in Matthew's side. As the sheriff stared up into the slowly dissipating smoke, he finally understood that Top Hat and the Mad Hatters had the last word after all.

The next two days passed in a nightmare of slowly, shifting images...smoke and fire licked Matthew's face and scorched his body. He cried out in fear and sorrow as he saw young Bob Higgins ride past grinning a death's head grimace, his white teeth nothing more than blackened nubs in a skull-like face.

"Oh, Bob," he muttered. "I am so sorry."

Bob just smiled and said, "That's alright, Boss. Come on! I want to show you something!"

Matthew roweled his horse, trying hard to catch up with his young deputy but his mount was afraid to follow. Bob's horse was awash in flames and snorted black smoke through wide, distended nostrils. Its fearful whinnies sounded like the cries of demons trapped in hell.

The sheriff moaned and shivered. Now he dreamed that he was a lost boy, once again stuck on a mountain top in a blinding blizzard, his only friend and companion an orphaned wolf cub. He was so cold his teeth chattered and Bandit whined anxiously as he stared into Matthew's face.

Doc Dearbourne gently scooted the wolf out of his way as he removed the bloody bandages from the sheriff's left side and murmured, "If he makes it past this fever, he has a fighting chance."

Roy frowned down at the young sheriff he had come to care for like a brother.

"What will it take, Doc? Do you need more medicine?" The deputy crushed his hat in his hands and glared outside at the racket the townsfolk and some of his fellow deputies were making in their efforts to clean up the small town that had almost burned to the ground in the conflagration.

Dearbourne sighed. "No. The bullet came out clean and I have given him enough opium to cope with the pain." He walked over to the woodstove that was blazing hot despite the afternoon heat.

Grabbing a cup of coffee, he added, "This young man seems to have given up. He suffered more than a gunshot wound, you know. With those broken ribs and the cut on his back that was starting to fester, the gunshot was just too much for his body to fight."

Roy stared down at Matthew again and bit his lip. Despite the fact that ten people—not including the bandits—had died, Matthew had pulled off a miracle. The town's citizens, all of whom would have perished had the sheriff not risked everything to save them from certain doom, were back home and rebuilding even as Matthew lay dying.

Coeur d'Alene sheriff, Mellon O'Brian, Travis, and a number of Spokane County deputies had ridden into town yesterday to help restore order. Even the Spokane County mayor and his retinue had arrived late last night to pay their respects and officiate in the funerals that were scheduled to take place tomorrow morning.

"Can he hear me?" Roy whispered.

"Maybe. It's hard to tell when patients go into this kind of shock." Dearbourne sighed again. "It wouldn't hurt. Maybe if he hears your voice, he'll make his way back to us."

"Can I try?" Iris Imes appeared in the doorway. Her eyes were red and puffy from the tears she had shed but she stood tall.

Roy gazed at the woman and remembered his own sweet wife and children as they tumbled out from the coach yesterday after the thirty-mile trip from Spokane Falls. He had been tempted to yell at Louise for undertaking such a long and expensive journey in order to fetch him home but his loved ones had screamed with joy at the sight of him and he recalled how his frozen heart had thawed as his family held him in their arms.

So, moving back, Roy murmured, "Yes, ma'am. If Matthew can hear anyone, I reckon it would probably be you."

Iris entered the room and sank down on the edge of

the bed as the deputy and the doctor stepped outside. The beautiful redhead took Matthew's hand and started telling him about the two new foals she had found at home after she escaped from the barn. She talked about the good yield on her wheat fields, and about the spotty new calves that ran after their mothers in the higher hills behind her ranch.

She told the young man that she needed a helping hand but his were the only hands she wanted on her body. She whispered in his ear that she had loved him for years and, once he got better, she would show him a thing or two about the marriage bed. She talked long into the evening and, finally, she curled up next to him on the bed and fell asleep, her fingers entwined with his. She didn't know it, but Matthew's fever broke soon after.

Slowly regaining consciousness, Matthew felt Iris's warm weight next to him. Looking down, he also saw Bandit staring into his eyes, panting. He fumbled around on the small table next to the bed and found a cup of water. Trying not to awaken the woman he loved, Matthew took a long drink and then allowed his wolf to climb up.

He fell asleep with those he adored nestled beside him.

34

A FINAL FAREWELL

TWO DAYS LATER, MATTHEW GOT OUT OF BED. HE WAS on the mend as was his town.

The new barn was already under construction, although under new ownership. An enterprising stable master had arrived from the Wenatchee area just after the funeral services concluded. He bought the land the burned barn sat on and took a big financial burden off the town coffers by footing most of the rebuilding cost himself.

The west end of the mercantile was being repaired, too, as smoke had damaged much of the outside walls. Even the small cemetery just outside the city limits was undergoing improvements. For one thing, it was growing rapidly and, for another, the Spokane Falls mayor had donated black, scrolled wrought-iron fencing brought in as a gesture of respect and sympathy from the citizens of that city.

The people of Granville had been tested but they

were survivors. They had to be. For the last three days, ever since the barn burnt and the outlaws were killed, the streets rang with shouts of joy and defiance. There were tears, yes, especially when so many good people were laid to rest at the mass funeral. Life went on, though, and now it was time to recover and rebuild.

Matthew had shakily made his way to the graveyard yesterday for the funerals but was still so weak from his wounds he was forced to take a chair like an old woman and pay his respects sitting down. He held his hat in his hands and remembered his deputies: Bob Higgins, Evan McCauley, and Murray Kotes.

He remembered sweet little Maggie who, more often than not, carried evidence of her family's trade on her flour-coated cheeks, nose and chin. And he silently thanked the tough and irascible Irish brothers, Davey and Joseph O'Connell, who had fought so hard against not being able to use their hidden poop-chute but had been so brave in trying to help subdue the outlaws.

He recalled Christopher Rundell, the kindhearted grocer who often gave his merchandise away for free despite his wife's constant nagging. In addition, he remembered Archie Almquist, the cobbler, who stuttered so badly he could hardly make himself understood but did such a fine job in boot and shoe repair that people as far away as Spokane Falls made a special trip into Granville for his services.

Finally, they lowered his aunt and uncle's coffins into the ground. Matthew thought he was prepared for it but, as memories of his Uncle Jon's many virtues swamped his mind, he thought his heart might break at the injustice of it all. His eyes got big as a huge gasp of grief threatened to overwhelm his senses and he started to tremble.

Many of the mourners let their tears fall as they remembered what good and kind people the Wilcoxes had been and gazed over at their young sheriff who visibly fought for control. They saw Doc Dearbourne bend over and whisper in Matthew's ear, then watched as he and Iris Imes helped the sheriff to his feet.

Matthew and Bandit walked over to the gravesite. As he grabbed a handful of dirt and tossed it into the open grave, the wolf raised its muzzle and howled. Bandit cried, and so did the people around him.

Ten miles away, a band of Indians paused what they were doing and listened as the wolf's howl carried over the hot air currents, scattering the flocking buzzards that looked down on them from high overhead.

Now Matthew walked outside and slowly heaved himself up onto his horse's back. His broken ribs were starting to heal but the gunshot wound in his left side still sang madly with a special brand of pain. Sitting still for a moment, Matthew caught his breath and then leaned over to let his wolf sniff the kerchief Top Hat once wore around his neck.

Bandit whined and took off to the east, nose to the ground. Matthew did not have much hope that his wolf could actually track down the outlaw as too many days had passed since Top Hat fled for the wolf to follow the man's scent. Yet he had to try.

A new arrest warrant had been issued against the gang leader and the sheriff knew that open season had just been declared; this was a "dead or alive" warrant. So, if anything, he was putting himself in a bounty hunter's crosshairs by going out without an escort.

Still, Matthew knew that the doctor would have forbidden him to go and Iris would have hog-tied him to his bed if she caught wind of his plans. As he lay in his bed the last few nights, however, Matthew knew he would never rest until his uncle's murderer… the boogieman, who had haunted his every waking moment since he was a boy, was apprehended.

The only citizen in town who heard his passing was the old dog, Muffin. Matthew had brought him home after the funeral and he whined as the sheriff and his wolf passed by the backyard of Matthew's house.

"Shhh, Muffin. Go to bed," Matthew murmured as they moved silently out of town, east into the foothills.

Matthew followed Bandit about nine miles at an easy walk and, at first, thought the wolf had a good scent to follow. Then he realized the animal was doing a big loop in front of him and whining…the trail was lost and Matthew gritted his teeth in frustration.

Suddenly Bandit stiffened and growled with alarm. Matthew looked ahead and spotted a number of vultures circling high in the air about five miles distant. He almost spurred his horse yet thought better of it as his whole body throbbed with increasing waves of agony and the chill of fever rising in his bloodstream.

Knowing that he was once again risking everything to find the outlaw who killed his uncle, Matthew smiled just the same with grim determination. Figuring that Top Hat had probably done away with yet another poor pilgrim in order to take everything the man held dear, he nudged his horse forward and prepared himself for the worst.

Coming up over a rise, Matthew held his pistol in his right hand and a rifle cradled crossways on his lap; Bandit was moving rapidly back and forth in front of his horse, panting with anxiety. Looking down, Matthew gaped at what met his eyes.

Top Hat lay spread-eagled on the ground twenty feet from the sheriff. He had been scalped and his genitals cut off and stuffed into his mouth like a bizarre snack. At least twenty-five arrows pierced the outlaw's body and Matthew could count numerous coup-cuts on Top Hat's arms, legs and feet.

A few yards away, an Indian war lance stood upright. On the warm afternoon breeze, Top Hat's newest beaver-skin hat—one Matthew knew was stolen from the mercantile in town—twirled in circles atop the weapon as though possessed by spirits of its own.

Matthew stared down at his old enemy's body and the back of his neck crawled. Looking around, he wondered if the attacking Indians were nearby as some of Top Hat's wounds seemed fresh. Yet, there had not been hostile Indians in these parts for many years; there were too many white men and U.S. soldiers in the area. Still, one never knew what might set tempers aflame and ruin a hard-earned truce.

Seeing no one, Matthew's shoulders sagged in relief and—almost in spite of himself—he did something so primal it was shocking. Letting his head fall back, he screamed out a loud howl of victory. Filled with anger, retribution and revenge, it made his wolf cower and the buzzards overhead scatter in alarm.

Matthew sat still for a bit and let his heart settle down. Then, calling Bandit to heel, he turned his horse around to head home when a dry branch snapped somewhere behind him. Bandit bristled and growled, staring past the brush into a stand of jack pines. Following the wolf's gaze, Matthew studied the tree line and saw an Indian sitting his pony about fifty feet away.

Red Bird stared across the gap that separated them and looked into Matthew's eyes. There was apology there...and defiance. Redbird knew he had stolen Matthew's quarry but he hoped young Slingshot would forgive him; the Indian could not move forward in life either until he killed the man who had murdered his little brother.

Brown eyes met green, held for another moment and—finally—blinked in understanding and forgiveness. Matthew removed his hat, bowed slightly, nudged his horse, and rode away.

FINALE: TO EVERY THING THERE IS A SEASON

Eleven months later, Matthew sat on the front bench of a wagon. Roy was sitting next to him, snapping the reins over the horse's rumps and whistling the wedding march as loudly as he could. He grinned obnoxiously as Matthew rolled his eyes and the deputy's children, sitting in the back, giggled at the sheriff's discomfort.

Matthew was getting married today and although his heart sang with joy and his sex-starved body tingled with suppressed desire and expectation, he had never liked a fuss. He only hoped that most of the people in town were far too busy to come to the wedding cere-mony. After all, it was harvest season and most of the farmers in the area were swathing wheat and hay from sunrise to sundown.

"You ready for this, Matthew?" Roy smirked. "Sure you don't need help figuring out what goes where?"

Matthew's cheeks turned red and he glanced over

his shoulders at Roy's kids. "Shhh! I will do just fine, Roy, if you don't mind!"

Roy and his family had moved to Granville not long after Matthew came home with news that Top Hat was dead. He cared for the young sheriff and knew Matthew needed help and someone he could trust since most of his force had died in the shoot-out. Louise and Iris had become fast friends and so had their children.

As far as Matthew was concerned, Roy was the big brother he never had. He looked up to the man, loved his family, listened to his advice and tried as hard as he could to stand up to his ribbing.

Sighing with embarrassment, Matthew muttered, "I hope you don't make me look like a fool in front of my sister and the preacher today."

Roy grinned. "Well, of course, I will!"

The weather was perfect for an outdoor ceremony and Matthew could see that a tent had been raised on the lawn in front of the house as Roy pulled the horses to a stop. Much to his dismay, he also saw close to a hundred people gathered inside that tent. They were grinning at him like a bunch of carnival clowns.

Roy murmured, "Thought you were going to get away with gettin' hitched without an audience, Sheriff? Fat chance of that happening!"

Matthew stared at the crowd as, one by one, they set down their drinks and plates and started clapping their hands. It seemed like everyone he had ever known was standing there; old friends and new acquaintances, all of them shouting his name and whistling in appreciation of his courage and fortitude. He wanted to melt into the ground or disappear in a puff of smoke, he was so embarrassed. But then Iris stepped out of the tent.

Wearing a cream-colored silk dress, her hair fell over her shoulders and down her back in wild profusion. Daisies were woven through the luxuriant strands and Bandit let out a yelp of joy, running to his new mistress with his tail whipping in undignified adoration.

Iris bent and caressed the wolf's graying ears then stood straight and tall, smiling at Matthew as he stepped down off the wagon. He still limped slightly from the bullet that had almost killed him but his green eyes gleamed when he looked at his future bride.

Enfolding Iris Imes in his arms, he kissed her with all his being as everyone wiped their eyes and cheered in happiness.

A LOOK AT DEADMAN'S FURY (THE DEADMAN BOOK II)

In 1892, Sheriff Matthew Wilcox learns that his wife's niece, Amelia Winters, has been abducted. Once more, he gathers his posse and hits the trail hunting outlaws. What he discovers shocks, dismays, and angers him: Amelia is only one of hundreds of women kidnapped and sold into sexual slavery.

An exotic auction is about to take place and time is of the essence. The sheriff and his posse are making things difficult for the criminals and a pile of money is at stake. The bandits realize, the sooner they can get rid of Sherriff Wilcox, the better.

But Matthew and his men won't go down easy.

In this much-awaited sequel to DEADMAN'S LAMENT, readers are in for another thrilling Western ride as these dedicated lawmen put their lives at risk seeking justice.

AVAILABLE NOW ON AMAZON

ABOUT THE AUTHOR

Linell Jeppsen is a writer of science fiction and fantasy. Her vampire novel, *Detour to Dusk*, has received over 44- four and five star reviews. Her novel *Story Time*, with over 130 4-and 5-star reviews, is a science fiction post-apocalyptic novel, and has been touted by the Paranormal Romance Guild, Sandy's Blog Spot, Coffee time Romance, Bitten by Books and 64 top reviewers as a five-star read, filled with terror, love, loss, and the indomitable beauty and strength of the human spirit. *Story Time* was also nominated as the best new read of 2011 by the PRG. Her dark fantasy novel, *Onio* (a story about a half-human Sasquatch who falls in love with a human girl), was released in December 2012 and won 3rd place as the best fantasy romance of 2012 by the PRG reviewers guild. Her novel, *The War of Odds*, won the IBD award for fantasy fiction and boasts 18 5-star reviews since its release in February of 2013. It also placed 2nd, as the best YA paranormal book of 2013 by the PRG.